What the Dog Knows

What the Dog Knows

SYLVIA McNICOLL

DUNDURN
PRESS

Publisher: Scott Fraser | Acquiring editor: Kathryn Lane | Editor: Susan Fitzgerald
Cover design and illustration: Laura Boyle

Library and Archives Canada Cataloguing in Publication

Title: What the dog knows / Sylvia McNicoll.
Names: McNicoll, Sylvia, 1954- author.
Identifiers: Canadiana (print) 2021039708X | Canadiana (ebook) 20210397101 |
   ISBN 9781459749894 (softcover) | ISBN 9781459749900 (PDF) |
   ISBN 9781459749917 (EPUB)
Classification: LCC PS8575.N52 W53 2022 | DDC jC813/.54—dc23

We acknowledge the support of the Canada Council for the Arts and the Ontario Arts Council for our publishing program. We also acknowledge the financial support of the Government of Ontario, through the Ontario Book Publishing Tax Credit and Ontario Creates, and the Government of Canada.

Care has been taken to trace the ownership of copyright material used in this book. The author and the publisher welcome any information enabling them to rectify any references or credits in subsequent editions.

The publisher is not responsible for websites or their content unless they are owned by the publisher.

Printed and bound in Canada.

Dundurn Press
1382 Queen Street East
Toronto, Ontario, Canada M4L 1C9
dundurn.com, @dundurnpress

High paws to all the dogs who walked through my head as I wrote this story. Mortie the Jackapoo, Worf the Australian cattle dog–boxer cross, Soji the Australian golden retriever, Piper the Bascottie, and Rosie the Bernedoodle. And to my grandchildren who walk them: William, Jadzia, Violet, Desmond, Scarlett, Hunter, Fletcher, Finley, and Ophelia.

Thursday, July 1:

Waiting for Relief

Do you ever regret something so hard that you play it over in your head a million times, with a million different endings except for the one that actually happened? Last week a car killed my dog, Diesel. My fault. I should have taken him babysitting with me — he loved my cousin, Luanne. I see myself making sure the gate latches properly behind me and that there are no holes under the fence Diesel can dig through to escape. I picture the Smart Car that hit him braking or scooting around him, and I see Diesel bounding after me, safe, ears flying behind him like flags in the wind.

Instead, here I sit on my aunt's stoop holding my fifteen-month-old cousin, rocking her back and forth, hoping the milk in her bottle will last till her mom comes home. July 1, Canada Day. We won't be picnicking at the beach like in other years. Everyone's working — "Service industry, what are you going to do?" Mom says — and it's too hot, same as every day since the beginning of June.

"Hot enough to fry an egg on the sidewalk," Dad used to say. Then last month he decided to prove it.

"Scientifically impossible," Mom said as she reached for the carton of eggs on the counter. "Besides, I'm the only one around here who ever fries any eggs."

Dad, teasing her and trying to make her laugh, I suppose, scooped the carton away from her and ran outside.

"You bring that back! I'm making breakfast."

Too late. The door slammed behind him. Diesel and I ran to watch as he knelt down on our walkway, removed one egg, and cracked it on the cement.

"You're wasting food!" Mom hollered from the window.

The egg collected dirt as it pooled into a groove. Dad cracked another on the driveway. That one ran down into the street.

"Stop it!" Mom yelled.

Diesel barked.

"Sunny side up," Dad called and broke open a couple more on the hood of the car. Those slid off.

The edges of one egg on the roof of our old Neon clunker finally turned white. "It's working!" I cheered.

"We don't have money for this!" Mom cried as that one slid down the windshield.

Dad should have stopped then and made pancakes for us all with the last two in the carton. Maybe then we could have just had a laugh together. But instead he went inside for tinfoil and a magnifying glass. That method might have worked in a couple of hours. But Diesel quickly licked those up as Dad scrubbed the rest off the car. Meanwhile, Mom packed Dad's clothes in a suitcase, which she pitched out the door.

"When you learn to act like a grown-up, you can come back."

If only he had made her breakfast instead. She would have forgiven the big screen Dad gave her for their anniversary earlier that morning — heck, she loves watching movies. We would still be together. Even Diesel, 'cause I wouldn't have had to babysit Luanne. Mom wouldn't have found that job at Donut Time, and she'd have been minding Luanne instead of me.

That's me imagining everything that month going a different way. I regret it all.

• • •

Today the sky looks as if one of those egg yolks is poaching right behind the cast-iron clouds. You can see the yellow through the cracks. Feels like a thunderstorm is coming, same as yesterday and the day before. The clouds grumble but they don't cry.

And I sure want to keep Luanne from crying, too.

"Shh, shh, Mommy's on her way." I stroke her damp forehead. Mostly she's a happy toddler, cooing and laughing, but with the heat she hasn't been able to nap all day. She's growing crabbier by the minute. Her skin feels feverish to the touch. The bottle's my last resort. She should be drinking from a sippy cup, but because she was born with a hole in her heart, we baby her a lot to keep her from getting too excited. Her mom's shift ended at two, and the watch Dad bought me now shows *THU July 01 3:30*.

"Everyone else uses a cellphone to tell time," I complained when Dad gave it to me on my last birthday. A red digital antique.

"This watch is water-resistant to two hundred metres," he answered. "You show me a phone like that."

"Yeah, well, you show me a watch I can use to text a friend. Besides, I'm not ever gonna go diving. I can't even swim." I acted as crabby as Mom. I regret that, too.

Today I smile at the watch. It makes me feel like a piece of Dad's dorkiness comes with me everywhere. I sure miss him living with us. Things are way too grown-up without him. The seconds spin by: *51, 52, 53* … Aunt Cathie should have been here half an hour ago.

Luanne's thick black hair lies flat and wet across her forehead. Her skin clams against my arms as her lips pucker out and in with a loud *pft, pft* sound. The milk is going down fast, and when it disappears, I'll be in for it. *C'mon, Aunt Cathie. Where are you?*

The road in front of Aunt Cathie's house steams. Maybe we can't fry eggs on the sidewalk like Dad says, but we can cook wieners on the street. Dog days of summer, Dad calls them. That's when Sirius, the Dog Star, rises in the sky with the sun. Can't see the star, just like I can't see my dog anymore.

Diesel was another birthday present from Dad. A surprise present for my tenth. Another thing that hadn't impressed Mom. "One more thing to look after," she complained. But who could resist a big-eyed, wobbly-pawed puppy? Not even Mom. Until he chewed socks, underwear, shoes, and even the door of the kitchen cupboard where we kept his treats. He upchucked on the couch and dug up the yard. Diesel grew big and strong and never stopped jumping on people. Mom blamed all that on Dad.

Seven days ago, my big teddy-bear dog lay at my feet, panting, ready to leap up if I even spelled the word *walk*. But then I left Diesel behind so I could babysit Luanne. Too much trouble to take him along. At least I should have put him inside where it was cooler, given him something to drink. Dad would have done that if he'd still been living with us.

Instead, Diesel took off out of the backyard. He was just coming after me. *If only I hadn't left him behind. If only, if only …*

Even Mom misses him. Her anger seems to have leaked out of her like air from a balloon. No reason for her to nag anymore. I can hear her in my mind: *Are you gonna walk that animal? Do I have to feed your dog? Why don't you brush him? His hair is all over the place.* Just like I can imagine the snuffling noises, the toenails clicking on the floor, the barks, the whimpers. Mostly our house just sounds quiet, angry turned sad. *Why didn't I take him that day? Why, why?*

Shifting Luanne in my arms, I lift my bare feet, ready to lower them onto Diesel's warm fur, and I swear I can feel the heaving of his chest beneath them and the thump, thump of his big heart beating *Everything is fine. Everything is fine.*

But that's my imagination acting up. The heat beneath my feet comes directly from the hard cement sidewalk.

Pft, pft, psht, psht! Luanne sounds like she's sucking on air now. Her brown eyes widen. I tip the bottle and prop up her hot body. "Hold on, hold on. She'll be here any minute." I shield my eyes to watch the corner bus stop. *Come on, come on, come on!* "Where's Mommy's bus?"

"There's a detour on Main Street." Morgan Hanson's razor-edged words cut the heavy air. Baby Luanne struggles to sit up.

Morgan Hanson, the tree-tall girl who lives across from Aunt Cathie, has snuck up on me. We've been not-friends since she moved to our block last year. We have nothing in common except the neighbourhood we live in and all the group projects we've had to do together. "You babysitting on a holiday?"

"What's it look like? It may be Canada Day but all my family is broke."

Morgan shrugs her twig-thin shoulders, looks around, and sighs. "Wanna come swimming with me after you're done?"

"That's okay. You go on ahead." Morgan knows from gym class that I can't swim. Yet all week she's been ragging at me to come with her to the pool, like she suddenly wants us to be besties.

"You're sad about the dog. I get it." Morgan tries again. "And you're cheap. But we're not even going to the pool. It won't cost anything at Hamilton Beach." Her pale eyes narrow like she's trying to read inside my head. She folds her long, branchy arms across her chest. "Wouldn't want you to wear the shine off your debit card."

I squint at her. "Diesel. My dog's name was Diesel." I swear Morgan just hangs around to make fun of me. "For your information, I don't even carry my debit card on me. All my money goes straight into the bank for my education." My parents can't save for anything, let alone medical school. Someday I'm going to be a heart surgeon and patch up a little kid's heart. A kid like Luanne.

"Whatever. The beach is free. And I heard they're giving away ice cream to the first two hundred fifty people. We should hurry."

"You don't have to wait for me. Not if there's a detour and Aunt Cathie's tied up for a long time." Part of me wants Morgan to hold back. Like a real friend would. Her parents are split up, so maybe we do have something in common, something she could help me with. Plus I imagine the beach at the lake, the white-winged sailboats skimming across blue waves. The sand will scorch my feet, but I can hop to the cool water and let it lap at my toes.

Imagination can sometimes be my biggest flaw. Probably I get that from Dad.

Morgan made fun of me enough in gym, windmilling her arms like mine when I tried the front crawl, snorting out water. But I can wade in as high as my waist without looking too stupid.

I squeeze my eyes closed, and I can see Diesel running and biting at the waves. *Clunk* — my heart hits my ribs so hard it hurts. I can't breathe.

"Lookie, lookie. Here comes Mama!" Morgan calls suddenly.

I open my eyes.

Morgan smirks. The large flecks of gold across her cheeks lift.

Luanne sits upright in my arms.

I haven't heard or seen the bus. But sure enough, there's Aunt Cathie strolling our way, big hips swinging beneath a plain aqua dress, her uniform for Maples Manor. Round and soft, she looks a lot like Mom. Except Mom always complains about needing to go on a diet. Aunt Cathie eats what she likes.

Luanne squirms, holding open her chubby arms and wailing. I set her down, and she toddles toward her mother.

Aunt Cathie waves as she draws closer.

Luanne steps faster. "Ma, ma!" For a kid who just learned to walk last month, she is lightning on legs.

Her face glowing from the heat, Aunt Cathie still manages to grin at her little girl. As soon as Luanne comes within arm's length, Aunt Cathie swallows her in a big hug, kissing her cheeks. "Mommy loves you," she coos into Luanne's ear. Then she turns to me. "Thank you, Naomi. Keeping Luanne at home with someone who loves her gives me such peace of mind."

I nod. "She didn't like the heat today." I hold up Luanne's empty bottle. "And that was the last of your milk."

"Wish I'd known." My aunt pats Luanne's back. "I could have picked some up on the way home."

True, but then she would have been even later. I should have just plunked Luanne in her stroller earlier and gone to the store myself. Maybe she would have fallen asleep. But then I would have had to use my own money for the milk, and who knows when Aunt Cathie would have paid me back. If ever.

"We could bring you some on the way home from the beach," Morgan suggests.

"Morgan, I didn't say —"

"Oh, that would be so helpful," Aunt Cathie answers before I can finish. She opens her purse and takes out her wallet.

Morgan grins at her. Then winks my way. She's forced me to come with her to the lake — putting one over on me again.

I give her an eye roll. Looks like my aunt's emptying her wallet, which means she doesn't have enough to pay me today. She owes me a couple weeks of babysitting money.

"Naomi, we're family," my mother will say if I complain. "You should be doing it for free anyway."

Still, I had plans for my summer before Aunt Cathie found this job at the Manor and Mom found hers at the donut shop. I signed up for swimming lessons but had to give them up to babysit Luanne. Shouldn't I get something for giving up my plans? Trouble is, everyone in our whole family is dirt poor.

"If there's enough change left, buy yourself a treat," Aunt Cathie tells me.

"Thanks," I say. 'Course there won't be. "See you in a bit." I head off toward my house.

"Where you going? The beach is this way," Morgan says.

"You go ahead. I have to get my bathing suit."

"Nah, you don't."

When I raise my eyebrows at her, she laughs.

"This is me showing you how to be cool. We go in the water in our undies and the restaurant people's eyes pop."

"I can't do that!"

"'Course you can't." She nudges my shoulder with a fist.

Oh right, she thinks she's funny.

"You kick off your flip-flops and go in your clothes, silly." Morgan strides ahead, long legs putting distance between us. "If you hurry, Simon will still be there."

"What do I care about Simon?" Dark hair and even darker eyes. Tall enough to see clean over me, like I don't exist — just the way all the girls in middle school don't see me. But they sure as all get-out see Simon. They wept when he graduated to high school a year ago. "How many people do you figure are ahead of us in line for ice cream?"

Thursday, July 1:

The Accident

Morgan turns and grins. Then she takes off walking again. She doesn't wait for me. "Let's just say you don't have time to go change," she calls over her shoulder.

I'm pretty sure she has no idea if there are crowds ahead of us or even for certain that Simon's at the beach. She's just playing me.

I should go straight to the store for the milk and then head home. Only, what else do I have to do right now? For a moment I see myself walking Diesel to the lake, where the cooler air blows against my skin.

I shake my head to clear that picture. I can't even imagine heading everywhere alone from here on in.

"Oh fine." I run to catch up. "Why do you want me to come anyway?"

She towers over me, making her look gawkier and me shrimpier. "You helped me bring my grades up last year. Only fair that I help you socialize."

"Can you make me taller or older? 'Cause that's what I really need to make friends." Having a December birthday makes me the runt of every class, and I just never grow. This year we're going into high school, and if I don't shoot up over the summer, I'll be everyone's mini-mascot.

"Can't make you taller, no."

"Well, then."

"But if you and me hang together, at least we won't be alone."

"I like being alone!" Leastwise I did when Diesel was alive. All I ever needed was my dog.

"Do you like looking like a loser, Naomi?"

"I don't care!" I answer. Hanging around with her may make me look even worse. She has a knack that way. Mimicking what I say or how I walk or bounce a ball, making me seem even more geeky. She didn't really do all that well in school last year even with my help. Never did what I told her. But for this one moment, I forget all that. I need someone to walk with, so I do a quickstep to keep up.

Down the long city block we go. Cars jam up in the street, pumping hot exhaust into the air and honking like a high school band.

"Hold up a sec." Morgan stops at the corner convenience store. "I'm boiling. Why don't we get a freezie now? Give me your aunt's money." She holds out her hand.

"It's for milk. Use your own. Besides, we're getting free ice cream."

"Whatever." She rolls her eyes. "Wait here for me." Morgan dashes into the convenience store while I stand outside in the heat. Not five minutes later she dashes out like someone is chasing her.

I start running just in case.

"Hang back!" she calls, and I turn just in time for her to throw me a rocket Popsicle.

I barely catch it. As she draws closer to me, I push it back toward her. "No thanks. I don't eat stolen goods."

"What are you talking about? I paid for this."

"You didn't have time."

"Yeah, I did. Threw down some coins. Didn't ask for the change." She nudges me. "Go ahead. You don't have to pay me back."

My tongue sticks to the roof of my mouth. Even though I don't believe her, I can't say no. Instead, I peel off the wrapper and taste the tangy ice. "Thanks."

"I've got your back, kid." It's what Morgan always says instead of *you're welcome*. Sure. Except the only bad mark I ever got was when I asked her to make a graph and a poster for our last presentation of the year. She used pencil crayon on leftover cardboard. Everything looked scribbled and messy. She didn't even get why I was ticked with her. Called me a teacher-pleaser peanut in front of everyone, and now that's what everyone calls me. Peanut, that is. Sometimes what I need most is someone to guard my back from her.

The three bars of my rocket, red, white, and blue, disappear in no time. I lick the melt from my hand as we continue together past the rows of townhouses, past the bars and restaurants.

The air starts to smell fishy. A short stroll along the shore road and we turn onto the beach, which is where it hits me like a tsunami.

An image of Diesel chasing a stick that I'd thrown for him.

I loved watching him gallop into the water, churning up waves like a motorboat. Then when the water turned deep, he calmly paddled toward the stick. He never brought it back. He just tore around on the beach, grinning and panting at me. I can see him. I want him back so badly.

My heart turns into an anchor, and my feet stutter to a stop.

"What's your problem now?" Morgan calls. "Look at that, they're all out there. Tom, Tara, Su-Ling, Brenna, Francesca … Simon." Her voice teases me with the last name. "All the cool kids from high school."

But everyone is not out there. Most people are celebrating at the other side of the lake, away from downtown. There are no boats and no dog, either. No long lineup for ice cream — that was Morgan messing with me again. Not even a flag in sight. Just a small plane dragging a pathetic

Happy Canada Day banner. But there is nothing at all happy about this Canada Day. A hot wind blows and the water wrinkles and folds roughly. Morgan runs ahead and I inch along slowly, dragging memories of Diesel with me.

When I reach the water's edge, I kick off my flip-flops and wiggle my toes in the wet muck. In the distance I can see those older kids who graduated ahead of us grouped at the foot of the long temporary dock that stretches from the beach in front of Zorba's Patio Bar. Like a mirage, their image shimmers in the heat. The dock can fit three boats on either side, but none are tied up there today.

As we get closer, I see Simon approaching the halfway point of the dock. His hair looks slick and wet already, and beads of water sparkle on his chest. He takes three long running strides and a powerful leap off the end. The water bursts open in applause.

Then Tom, the gangly, red-haired goof, runs and jumps. A big cannonball splash that drenches the girls. They shriek. One by one, they jump in after him. Francesca with cat-like grace. Tara, beach-waved hair flying. Brenna, pouty lips open in a squeal. Finally Su-Ling, holding her nose and giggling. Long-haired, long-legged, smooth-skinned girls. Everyone looks great; everyone can swim.

I desperately want to do that, to be part of all that fun. To belong. The water can't be that deep, can it? Not if they're bobbing up so fast and running back up the dock again.

Tara waves. "Come on in. The water's fine!"

One of them is talking to me?

"Not cold at all," Tom calls. Simon's joker sidekick can't exactly be trusted on matters like this, not if there's the possibility of drawing a laugh from the look of ice-water shock on the face of someone he's fooled into jumping.

The water has to be over their heads. I need to be able to stand. Can I just wade in on my own? Lie down in the water, stomach in the mud, the way Diesel used to? The way he still does in my head, when I regret hard enough.

Will they leave me be if I just do my own thing? Of course they will. I'm just the peanut from middle school, after all. Who pays any attention to me? They see straight over me.

"Last one in is a rotten egg!" Morgan taunts as she runs up the dock, leaving me behind on the water's edge. She jumps in.

A peanut and a rotten egg.

I step in slowly, ridges of sand soft under my feet. Last September I took swimming in gym like everyone else, till the city closed the pool. What did I learn? No running in the pool area. That's it. The budget was cut before I even mastered treading water. The teacher joked that I needed more fat on my body to float. "You're just too big a klutz," Morgan said. Both had a point.

So I signed up for lessons this summer, then had to drop out to babysit Luanne.

"I'll teach you myself. It's not that hard," Dad promised when I told him. But I knew I couldn't depend on him, especially when he explained how he learned: "My older brothers threw me into the canal and I had to sink or swim."

If he could learn in that deep, murky waterway where all the ships dumped their oil, surely I can learn in this clean lake.

I wade in past my ankles. Colder now. My feet turn into Popsicles. I will keep going till the water reaches the top of my knees and no farther. Can't get my shorts wet, after all.

Simon and Tom hoist themselves back up on the dock. The long-legged ones run past me out of the water, then back onto the dock.

A shriek from Morgan. Her feet pound the boards before she leaps off a second time. There's a sound like glass panes shattering and more shrieks when she comes up. "Hurry. It's fun!" Her voice sounds different. Is jumping in really that fun? Or is she just putting one over on me?

"Come on, Peanut. You can do it," Simon calls.

"'Course I can do it. I just don't want to," I mutter as I wade in deeper. A wave splashes over my knees. Another, even higher. *Whoosh!* I suck in my breath. Now my butt is wet. Great. Looks like I've peed myself.

"The water carries you up if you let it," Dad told me last time he tried to teach me. I was four years old. He held me by the strap of my bathing suit, but then he let go.

I sank. The water was calm and I sat on the bottom, believing I could breathe it. I could live there. A magic blue sea world. I never wanted to come back up. But Dad ripped me out of that world after I choked on my first breath of it. Back on land, I coughed out all the water. "You have to stretch your arms and kick your legs, Naomi!"

Is that all it takes? Last September, I couldn't make my legs and arms work at the same time. Coordination. "Puny *and* clumsy." Morgan shook her head and rolled her eyes.

But I'm almost a whole year older now. Maybe things have changed. I slosh through the water toward the dock, ready to try.

Morgan scrambles up on the dock. "Let's jump together." She holds out a dripping wet hand.

I shake my head. Not going to trust her. No free ice cream, and she for sure stole that Popsicle, too. Under my own steam, I climb onto the dock and walk to the edge. From this angle the lake looks as though it reaches toward eternity.

"I'll catch you," Simon teases from the water. Big-armed Simon holds me in his eyes, smiling. He makes all the girls love him like that. Even peanuts like me.

I wait some more. And watch as all the kids climb up and leap.

Morgan jumps in a third time.

Should I do it, too? It looks so easy.

I can feel the motion in the dock. I hear a rumble. Rock against a post? Thunder in the sky?

I inhale deeply. Thick, heavy, hot air. Morgan waves to me. She swims to shore. I jump.

I never close my eyes or pinch my nose. As I hit the icy water, my breath freezes to my heart. A wave flings me upside down and white bubbles rush up all around me. Down, down through the murky dark. The back of my head knocks against a rock. *Ow!* I tumble over. Which way is up?

Hurry, you have to get air. Something pounds hard and fast inside me. *Maybe I can breathe down here,* the four-year-old inside me says. *No, no, no! You have to get real air.* I see brighter grey in one direction and flap my arms and legs to get to it.

They still don't work together.

Lines of fire shoot down the inside of my chest. *Need to breathe, soon.* Finally, my nose breaks through the water. Then my mouth. I gasp. *Whomp!* Another wave flings me under. No chance to grab that breath.

I push one arm through the water. My hand reaches for the sky, my fingers clawing desperately in the air. Another wave hits me hard like a punch. I sink again. The fire licks at my throat now.

I kick my legs hard and break the surface again, mouth first.

I open it to catch a breath and yell for help but instead — *whoosh!* — water floods into my mouth.

I flail and sink. Flames fill my head, exploding into a million white lights behind my eyes. Is this what dying feels like?

"Naomi!" I hear Morgan call from somewhere in the distance. "Someone help me. I don't know where Naomi went!"

Morgan, I should have trusted her.

Friday, June 25:

Waking Up Last Week

Ow, ow, ow! I wake up with rocks pounding against the inside of my skull. I roll to my side. I'm on some kind of hard patio stone. I drop my hands from my face and sit up, gasping in oven-hot air. Where's the sand? Where's everyone?

I jumped in the water. Morgan must have found me and dragged me to the beach. I can picture the crowd gathered around my body stretched out on the sand. Did she perform artificial resuscitation?

Only, there's no one around. Instead of sand, brittle brown grass stretches in front of me all the way to a rickety fence. Our backyard.

"Rouff! Rouff! Rouff!"

Man, that barking sounds so loud, like it's bouncing on the inside of my head. *Ow, ow, ow!*

Hot air puffs fast and heavy against the back of my neck.

I inhale the cooked-hamburger smell of dog's breath and turn — *ow*, too fast for my aching head — and smile. "Diesel? You're alive?"

I blink. Pinch my arm, hard, and see the white line from my nail form on my skin. I can feel it, too. So I can't be dreaming.

Diesel's milk-chocolate muzzle opens into a panting grin. I throw my arms around him. Drool drips onto my shoulder. Wet. I feel that, too. "Yuck!" My nose wrinkles but my heart smiles.

"Drooling relieves stress." I hear the words, mellow and soothing like hot chocolate. Only, the hot chocolate bubbles inside my head. My imagination has really kicked into high gear.

"Drooling is how dogs relax." More words. If *I'm* thinking them, why are they in someone else's voice?

Diesel's body language matches that hot-chocolate voice. His wide pink tongue washes over me.

Then he bounds away, zigzagging across the yard. Joy and energy, despite the heat. The voice turns loud and happy. "Drooling is dog yoga." Again, not my thoughts, not my voice. Diesel wags his tail. He barks.

"Are you talking inside my head?" My nerves vibrate like plucked guitar strings. *Am I dead?* I freeze. That has to be it. *Morgan never did find me. Never pulled me out of the water.* I breathe in deeply to get some air. In, out, in out, too quickly. I feel my head floating. *How can I breathe if I'm dead?*

Don't worry! You're not dead.

But I never asked that question out loud. Who's answering my thoughts? My heart drums.

That hot-chocolate voice soothes. *Look at me. Watch me. More dog yoga.* Diesel faces me and lowers himself on his front legs, a move he's done hundreds of times when he wants me to play. *Downward dog*, his voice growls inside me.

Not only is he talking, he's hearing my thoughts and answering me. I hold on to the sides of my throbbing head. Dad said a Smart Car ran over him. But he's standing right in front of me; Dad must be wrong.

"You're supposed to be dead," I tell Diesel.

I came back to save you. His thick tail fans the air, and he pushes his head against me. *Pat me! Calm, calm.*

I finger his silky ears, and my breathing slows. "So, I bumped my head and now you talk inside of it?"

You always understood me.

"Not this clearly, I didn't."

I couldn't make you pay attention. This way I will.

The back door of the house creaks open and my mother steps onto the porch.

"Naomi, what are you doing on the ground fussing with that animal? It's ten thirty already. You're going to make Cathie late if you don't leave right this minute."

What do I do now?

Don't tell the alpha female!

Like I ever would. Voices in your head, is that schizophrenia? I don't know what's going on, only that I will have to stall for time until I do. "Something happened. I … I passed out," I tell her. "Hit my head."

"What?" Even as she rushes down the stairs toward me, Mom scolds, "Running in the yard with that darned dog in this heat! No wonder."

It's not my fault. That other voice in my head again. Diesel whimpers. *I'm here to save you, Naomi.*

Mom holds my chin in one of her hands. "Where does it hurt?"

"Here." I point to the fiery centre of pain at the back of my head.

She touches the spot gently.

"Ow!"

"You've got a bump the size of an egg."

Could a head injury make me imagine drowning so clearly?

Calm, calm. Don't worry about the before. Live in the now, the hot-chocolate voice says in my head.

"Let's go in and ice that." Mom helps me up and holds my elbow as we climb the porch steps.

Diesel scrambles up behind us. *Coming with you, too. I need to stay close to save you.*

He slumps down near my feet as Mom sits me down at the kitchen table. Clicking her tongue, she takes a bag of corn out of the freezer and holds it against the bump. "I can't afford to lose a shift at the donut shop," she grumbles. "Here." She places my hand over the bag. "You hold it."

My fingers press the icy kernels into the pain. The pounding fades to a soft drumming. "Why does everyone have to work on Canada Day anyway?"

"What are you talking about?" Mom turns on the tap and fills a glass with water. "It's the twenty-fifth of June. Canada Day's not until next week."

"What?" I hold my head, feeling woozy for a second.

Mom hands me the glass. "Here, drink!" She watches as I down it. "How many fingers?" She holds up her hand in front of my eyes.

"Five, Mom." June 25 — there is something special about that date. This all feels so familiar. And yet different.

I didn't run into the street! Diesel's voice inside me. Growling, deep and rumbly, like coffee brewing.

June 25. Of course. The first day of my life without Diesel. The day after that Smart Car killed him.

I learned my lesson, he barks again.

Déjà vu? I squeeze my forehead with my other hand and swallow hard. Everything swirls.

Déjà vécu, Diesel's voice answers. *We have already lived it.*

How can we have already lived this? Wait a minute, you speak French? It's all too much. *You're not even a poodle!*

Mom stares at me. "You don't look good. I wonder how long you were passed out."

I shake my head. I want to throw up. Did I live the future in a hallucination? That clearly? Am I psychic? Did I see my own death?

Diesel lays his head over my feet. *Calm, calm. The now, the now.*

"We should run you over to the hospital. Maybe when your father gets here. Where is that man?" Mom peers out to the front of the house.

They'll put me in the psych ward if I tell them about the dog voice in my head. "Do I have to go there?" I ask. *They'll give me something to make it go away.*

"To the hospital? If you have a concussion —"

"No. I mean to Aunt Cathie's. Can't she just bring Luanne over here?" Last time through this, I went over there. Can I change things, even a little?

Baby Cheerios? Bring her here! Yes, yes. Diesel's tail thumps hard.

Luanne always tosses him cereal bits.

Mom squints into my eyes. "I don't see how that's any better."

"I won't need to walk in the heat, for one." Plus I don't ever want to take chances with Diesel again. This way he will stay safe; he won't have to chase after me. "All my stuff is here. We have the big screen. I can just lie on the couch." *And sort things through.*

Diesel lifts himself and leans his head on my lap.

"Yes, but Luanne's crib is over there." Mom digs her fists into her hips.

The lump at the back of my head turns numb. I put down the bag of frozen corn and rub Diesel's silky ears. *Yes, yes,* that voice soothes in my head.

"I'm feeling a lot better already."

Mom's mouth bunches. Of course she doesn't want to leave me alone with Luanne. If anyone in our family had any kind of money, she wouldn't worry about missing a few hours of work. She'd stay home with me.

The phone rings, and when she picks up, I can tell it's my aunt. Mom explains the situation to her and my solution. "My shift starts later. I have to leave by eleven. If she doesn't look better, I'll ask James to stay with her."

At the mention of Dad's name, I wonder about him and Mom. Is it possible that they're still together? That the whole breakup was a part of that super-vivid hallucination?

If only Dad hadn't bought Mom that widescreen or had at least stopped cracking eggs all over the place, Mom wouldn't have thrown him out, I'm sure of it. He must regret that to his core. If regret changes anything, it should change that.

I hear the front door open. One of Diesel's ears springs up. His tail thump-thumps. *Alpha Male!*

"Hello in there!" Dad whistles as he continues into the house. Whistling Dad means cheerful Dad. He strolls into the kitchen, grinning.

Diesel barks hello and runs toward him. I stand up and rush toward him, too. Diesel and I collide.

"I'm so happy to see you, Dad." I hug him and Diesel jumps on him.

The way Dad reacts will tell me what's up. If he lives with us still, he will eyeball me and chuckle, then say something like "Get up earlier and you'll see me more often."

Instead, Dad hugs me too tightly. Desperately. "Me, too, Naomi."

Darn.

Diesel wags his whole body.

Hello. Hello, Alpha Male. The words bark in my head. Diesel flips over, in what looks like a breakdance move. *Pat me. Pat me. It is good for your blood pressure.*

My brain feels like a dried-up sponge. I swallow hard, return to the table to grab my glass, and go to the sink to refill it with water. I'm imagining things, have to be. All that stuff, the dog dying, me jumping off the dock, drowning — crystal clear as it is in my head, none of it can be real. After all, I'm here. The white pinch mark from my fingernail has turned blue now.

Still, why do I hear Diesel's thoughts inside my head?

I will talk you through this. Everything will be fine. I can save you.

I gulp more water down, then take a breath. Mom has to leave soon. I need to pull myself together. What time is it anyway? I check my watch and start to shake.

Mist and droplets of water cling to the inside of the crystal. I tap the glass, but the display reads *THU July 01 4:30*. Next Thursday. My brain swirls. Can this be part of some brain damage thing? I blink a few times. The date stays the same. I look around, but no one seems to notice my confusion. Only the dog.

The time counter stopped. Diesel tilts his head, sending his thoughts into mine. *Our life counter. Stopped just for now. We can make it start again after I save you. Don't worry!*

The Here and Now

But it's not the watch I worry about. While I tap at the buttons at the side to reset the date and time, Dad continues talking and patting Diesel's belly. "Diesel, you sure are something."

Diesel flips back over and licks at his lips. *I love you.* He licks at his lips some more. *I miss you and our games of tug and ball.*

Dad always said that lip-licking was Diesel trying to answer us. Mom would argue that he was just hinting for treats.

Today Dad just says, "Good dog," and Mom doesn't argue.

Dad reaches into his back pocket for his wallet and turns to Mom. "Got your support money."

They are definitely still separated. Double darn.

Don't be sad. Diesel whimpers as he walks over to my chair. *We are alive.* He puts a heavy paw on my knee and pants happily. *Right here, right now.*

I shake my head and stare at the watch face. When I fell in the backyard, the watch must have taken a hard knock that somehow changed the date and time. Easy enough to happen, leaning on a button too long.

But what about the moisture trapped inside the face?

Humidity, heat, who knows?

I look at Diesel. *What do you mean, life counter?*

Diesel whines a short one-note, then jumps on me, knocking the table. *I can save you. We can save the pack.*

"A demolition derby, that's what that dog is," Mom grumbles.

Diesel groans and drops back under the table.

"Mom, did you happen to see a Smart Car around yesterday?" I ask, trying to sound casual.

Diesel bumps my leg with his head, hard. Then he puts his head down and I feel the vibration of his growl against my ankle.

"One of those little toy cars? No one around here drives those," Dad answers.

"Actually, I did see a young girl in one at the drive-thru. They must be very economical to drive." She shoots Dad a look. For sure, his old clunker is not.

A Smart Car. Darn, it can't all be just a strange dream.

"Rouuff, rouuff, rouuff!" *We will keep each other safe!*

"I swear that dog is trying to talk to you, Naomi." Dad shakes his head as he hands Mom some bills — fifties, twenties, tens.

OMG — if Dad only knew! I try one last time to make sense of what happened.

"Dad, did you take Diesel to the vet yesterday?"

"No. Is it time for his yearly checkup or something, Naomi? 'Cause I haven't even been for my own physical yet."

"No. I meant, did Diesel have an accident, hurt himself somehow, and need to go to the animal hospital?"

Diesel barks sharply. *No, no, no!*

"Look at that! You're upsetting the dog with all this vet talk." Dad squats down near Diesel. "C'mon, I'd have told you. Heck, I would have had to borrow from you to pay the bill." He rubs the tip of Diesel's ear. "This dog should be in the movies. Could make us a fortune."

"Sure," Mom drawls as she counts the money. "The kind where the dog chases something and throws over a buffet table."

"Well, exactly. Every dog movie has one of those scenes," Dad says.

"Hmph." Mom's lips lift just a little. An almost smile. This is good. Since Dad was let go from the steel company, Mom never smiles at anything he says.

Diesel sprawls underneath the kitchen table, nose between his paws, moon-eyed with innocence. *I'm a good, good dog.* His eyes look straight into mine, a sliver of white showing. *Aren't I?*

"We wouldn't have to train Diesel to behave badly," Mom says.

Diesel whines a longer two-note. First one starts high and blends into the second lower one.

"Diesel is a good, good dog." I repeat Diesel's thought outside my head.

Neither of them listens to me. Instead, Mom squints at the money in her hand. Then counts a second time.

A memory comes to me suddenly, the before: Mom yelling at Dad 'cause I can't stop crying over Diesel. "This is all your fault," she says. She's crying, too. Dad ends up leaving.

I blink hard. Today is different, all in a good way. Diesel is alive, nothing to argue about.

"Sorry, I'm a little short this week," Dad tells Mom. "I can make it up to you in September."

Diesel shifts under the table. *Oh, oh! Alpha Female grows angry!*

Mom frowns. "This won't be enough!"

Here and now is enough. We have toast and warm meat!

Okay, now that's definitely Diesel thinking in my head.

Blankets, toys! Walkies. We have our pack. Shelter!

"Why does money have to matter so much around here?" My voice comes out whiny. I didn't drown. Diesel's alive!

Mom stares at me.

"Well?" I try again. "Money's not the most important thing, after all."

Mom looks at Dad, shakes her head, and turns to me,

sighing. "Because we're behind on rent. The landlord wants us to leave."

No shelter? Diesel asks.

My breath catches. "I'll give you the money in my bank account."

"No!" Mom snaps.

"Where will we go, then?"

Mom crosses her arms in a roadblock and glares at Dad.

I would like to live with Baby Cheerios, Diesel says. *Our pack could grow and be stronger.*

I think about Diesel's words for a moment. Then reason out loud: "We don't need a house all to ourselves. Aunt Cathie struggles by herself with Luanne — Uncle Greg working in Fort McMurray and all."

Mom and Dad both stare at me.

Diesel's tail thumps his applause.

"Since Dad lives with Uncle Leo now, why can't we move in with Aunt Cathie?"

Dad's eyebrows lift.

"You'd share a room with Luanne?" Mom asks. "You babysit so much as it is."

"I could sleep in the basement. We could fix it up. It's cooler down there anyway."

"Luanne would be around all the time."

"We're family," I answer.

It takes a moment to sink in. Then Dad's mouth widens into a grin. "Just listen to my girl. Did you ever hear such great problem-solving skills?"

The heat of Mom's anger crackles in her words. "*She* has ambition. That solves problems. Did you apply to Willow Farms?"

"Not yet," Dad murmurs down into his chin.

Willow Farms sounds nice, like Dad would be feeding chickens and milking cows, and half our neighbourhood works there. But really it's a meat-packing plant. Truckloads of pigs with their noses pressed to the grates travel past on the main road to Willow Farms.

Morgan's father works there. He trains new employees now, ever since he lost three fingers in one of their machines. I would worry if Dad got a job at Willow Farms. Still, he needs to do something to make Mom like him again. He just shorted her on our rent money, after all.

What can I do to help him look better in her eyes?

"Hey, Dad. Can you give Mom a lift to work today? She's running behind on account of me knocking my head."

"You hurt your head, Naomi?" Dad looks closer at me. "How?"

"Playing in the hot sun too long with that dog," Mom grumbles.

As if my heatstroke is Dad's fault because he gave me Diesel. As if Diesel's running into the street was his fault. His fault, his fault. Same argument, only shifted slightly.

Diesel whimpers.

I am a good dog. I can save the whole pack.

"Passed out and gave herself a bump on the head," Mom continues her grumble.

"You sure you're not concussed?" Dad asks. "Should I run you over to the hospital?"

"Rawf!" Diesel barks.

"Shush. No one's asking you," Mom tells him.

I shrug, not sure at all. There seems to be a whole other movie track running in my head. And a dog talking. Does that go along with being concussed? If Dad takes me to emergency, will the hospital release me again? Not if I tell them about the dog voice.

Maybe they'll drug me so I won't hear Diesel anymore. But I like talking with my dog.

"I'm fine," I say and change the subject. "If you drive Mom, she can save her bus fare." A penny saved is a penny earned, Mom told Dad when she refused to get internet. Well, three dollars saved must be three dollars earned, then.

"I'd be happy to drive you. Heck, if there was a bus route to my job at Western Tire, I'd give you the car."

"Whoa! Did you hear that, Mom?"

Mom scorches him with a look, and really, I don't believe him, either. He could never give up the blue machine.

She speaks to him in a forced normal tone. "I would appreciate a ride. So I can get to Donut Time on time."

Dad points to her and chuckles. "Well, we'll get you there ahead of Donut Time!"

Circle sweets with holes, so delicious. Diesel knows Mom brings day-olds home all the time. *My kibble is dry and tasteless.*

"Hey, Dad, Mom can probably score you a free coffee and donut. Right, Mom?" She needs to smile. Everyone loves when Mom smiles. Will those lips lift?

"I could use my employee discount." She raises an eyebrow at me, touches my head. "Are you sure you're all right?"

The front door opens. Diesel barks.

Mom turns toward the hallway. "That will be Cathie and Luanne."

She frowns as she studies my face.

"Don't worry, I'm feeling a lot better." It's true — no rocks in my head, no drumming.

Baby Cheerios! Diesel's tail thumps.

Just confusion.

When Aunt Cathie walks in, I open my arms to Luanne. "I'm so glad to see you, baby," I say as she snuggles into them, clutching her old worn-out stuffed monkey.

"My, my, I'm lucky Luanne gets such loving care," Aunt Cathie says. "Makes my life so much easier, Naomi, knowing you're looking after her."

My heart hammers. Those words sound familiar. I know I've heard them before. Or something close to them. *Keeping Luanne at home with someone who loves her gives me such peace of mind.* Just a little different. My *déjà vu*, or *déjà vécu*, seems to be shifting. I take a couple of deep breaths. Maybe I can change destiny, if that's what that drowning was all about.

I'll start with the most important thing. Everything else can go the same, but Diesel can't die. I won't let him. I'll keep him away from Smart Cars — heck, from any motorized vehicles. What's the point of having this kind of vision if I can't change the most vital part of my future?

"You do look a little off. Are you sure you'll be okay?" Aunt Cathie asks.

I nod. "We'll watch television and Luanne will go for a nap. I'll be fine."

Dad offers to drive Aunt Cathie, too, which is a good thing. Two bus fares saved; so many pennies earned. I grab Luanne's hand and lead her to the window to watch them leave. Dad unlocks the car doors and they all climb in, Mom in the front and Aunt Cathie in the back.

"Woof!" Diesel jumps up, leaning his front paws on the window ledge. *The alphas of our pack are leaving!*

"It's okay. They'll be back." Sounds like I'm explaining to Luanne as I hoist her up on my hip, holding her hand and waving it at the tempo of Diesel's wagging tail. Sounds almost sane. I watch out the window, hoping for some kind of sign that things will be all right. Better, even. I knock at the glass, wanting Mom and Dad to see us. Maybe Mom will chuckle and nudge Dad. They'll share a moment. If they do, I'll know I can save them, too.

Then I see my sign. The corners of Mom's lips turn up. Who can resist Luanne's chubby arm and dimpled hand raised in the air? Not Mom. She smiles a full-toothed grin. She turns to Dad and points back at us. It even looks like she's laughing. I wish I could hear her through the two panes of glass separating us.

But Dad will be able to, that's the main thing. Dad taps the horn and Luanne squeals and kicks her legs happily.

"Things are looking up, Diesel, I can tell. Maybe we *can* bring Mom and Dad together again. You and me."

Alpha Male and Alpha Female fight. But we should not exile our alpha. Diesel gives a long one-note whine, inside my head or out, I can't tell which.

I pat him. "Nothing we can do about that this minute. For now, let's just go and watch some TV."

Friday, June 25:

Playing It Safe

After spending some of his severance money from the steel company on a giant-screen TV, Dad got Uncle Leo to help him secretly set it up in the basement. On the morning of their anniversary, Dad cozied up to Mom as she opened her card. "A theatre room?" she squealed. I thought she was loving it.

"We can enjoy movie dates right here in the house." He led her down the stairs so she could see. I followed behind.

Mom gasped. The screen was huge. Then she pushed him away. "You should have saved that money for a rainy day."

"It's always raining at this house," Dad grumbled.

"All the more reason not to install a movie theatre in the cellar," Mom snapped. Then she stomped back up the stairs to make breakfast.

She would have come around. I know she would have. She loves watching the old movies Dad brings home from the library because we can't stream new ones on the internet. But it was so hot and sticky that day.

Hot enough to fry eggs on the sidewalk. Or not, as Dad's experiment proved.

So Dad never did get to enjoy his theatre room.

But today we sure do. Down here, the air feels cool and smells like wet, salty earth. Luanne and I stretch out on the L-shaped couch. Diesel sprawls on the carpeted cement floor, belly up, feet in the air.

Even though it's not a finished basement, and she says she's not into the big-screen thing, Mom has fixed up the area nicely. She covered up the cement wall on either side of the screen with purple thrift-store drapes, and the other exposed-brick walls she painted white. If it weren't for the salty basement smell I could imagine we were in the movie theatre. The room feels almost like one of those new ones with the big, comfy seats I've heard about.

I thumb the remote to get to my channel.

Today, *Super Canines* is on. We watch as a chocolate-coloured dog named Titan sprints through an obstacle course of tunnels, springboards, and hurdles.

"Disie!" Luanne bounces on my lap.

Diesel flips over and leaps onto the couch. *How can I help?* He licks Luanne's face.

"Check it out, Diesel. That dog could be your twin." With one ear up, the other down, Titan runs to sit by his owner's side.

You called me for that? Not treats? "Arouff!" Diesel snatches a pillow and leaps down again.

"You can't eat that!" I yank the cushion from his teeth and white fluff drifts through the air.

Pillows are dog chewing gum. He yawns and ends it with a whine. *I'm so bored.*

I ignore Diesel's complaint. "Watch this dog and learn."

Flat pictures don't interest me. "Arouuff!"

The announcer declares Titan the overall champion of the National Agility Games. I glance Diesel's way. "No reason you couldn't be a champion, too. You have the same bodies."

I am already a champion. He sneezes out some pillow fluff. *Running through tubes and jumping on things is useless. There is no prey.*

Titan's owner takes a bow while her dog sits quietly raising one paw. Then, as they make their way over to the announcer for a post-game interview, he step-bounces alongside the woman in the same dingo style Diesel uses.

The announcer asks the owner about Titan's breed and she explains that Australian cattle dogs are intelligent, loyal family dogs who make great herders.

"See that, Diesel. You're intelligent and loyal."

I know. Right now I am busy cleaning. Diesel licks at his dog bits.

"Before you go," the announcer finally says, "could you give the viewers at home your most important tip to get a dog to behave?"

"Sure. The answer is easy. Exercise, exercise, and more exercise. If I don't give Titan jobs to do, he gets bored and into mischief."

Walkies? Walkies? Diesel asks inside my head. He has to be listening to the show a little.

"Too dangerous," I answer out loud. *We have to keep you safe.*

I won't run in the street. I know better.

"No!"

Then I will amuse myself.

Diesel latches onto Luanne's stuffed monkey. She giggles as he growls and grins at the same time, giving the monkey a shake.

"Exercise," I repeat as I snatch the toy away from him. "Not destruction. How can I exercise you inside?"

Throw the pillow with eyes! He jumps on the couch and tries to get the monkey back.

I tuck the monkey under one arm and pick up the remote to flip away from the canine competition, figuring Luanne and Diesel aren't watching anyway. As I surf the channels, a scene stops me. It's a monitor with a black background and a green line jumping up in peaks in time to a heartbeat. The beat intensifies, then stops as the green line flattens. A piercing beep sounds. I lift my thumb off the remote.

"Sajan Andrews suffered a massive heart attack and died for five minutes." On screen a surgeon holds paddles to somebody's chest. The heartbeat begins again. "Listen as he talks about his near-death experience."

He has my attention. My drowning felt like a near-death experience. Maybe we're really dead and I'm dreaming we're alive. A hot shiver shoots up my spine.

Diesel yips. *We aren't dead.*

What do you know? You're a dog.

Dogs know plenty.

Explain it to me, then.

I have already told you. We are not dead. You are not dreaming.

But what about my drowning? The watch?

He whines. *When you need me, I can save you.*

Well, right now I'm concentrating on saving you. I turn to the near-death show hoping for some answers.

Sajan Andrews speaks: "There was a whooshing sound. And a force tugged me toward a huge blinding-white beam of light. Almost like a tunnel."

Doesn't sound anything like what happened to me, but it gives me an idea of how to exercise Diesel. I grab the emergency flashlight off the wall and shine it around the floor. Diesel immediately leaps after it.

"Rawf, rawf!" *I can catch the dancing star!*

Luanne squeals, slides off the couch, and toddles after him.

Sajan Andrews continues: "There was no bottom or top on the tunnel of light but the outside edges glowed. I felt at peace."

In my drowning vision, when the waves pounded all the breath from me, there was never any tunnel of light. I can't be dead, right?

Diesel stops chasing the light and jumps up on the couch. *We are not dead. I'm sure. I know.*

My stomach growls; Diesel has to be right. Dead people don't get hungry, do they?

Must be time for lunch. I check my watch. No steam or moisture now, but the readout has returned to *THU July 01 4:30.*

No, no, no. I'm sure I set it right before. *You said it would start again.*

It will, when we are safe.

But we are safe, aren't we? My fingers tremble as once again I press the buttons on the side of the watch to bring the date back to June 25. The time on the television screen reads 12:30. I fix the time readout, too. Do I have to save my change somehow? Like on a computer?

"Rouff." *We must stay alive.*

What do you mean? I'm breathing quickly, hyperventilating. But Diesel doesn't answer. My stomach rumbles again. Hunger's making me dizzy and panicky. "C'mon, lunchtime, everybody!"

Diesel springs up the stairs at the L-word, and I scoop Luanne into my arms and follow. I set her down in the kitchen, take bread from the cupboard, and stick four slices in the toaster. This is taking too long!

Calm, calm. Diesel pants at me, holding my eyes with his for a moment. *Drool with me.*

I take a breath. *Humans don't drool to relax.* Instead, I grab some baby carrots from the fridge, stick one in my mouth, and chew quickly, hoping a vegetable will stop my panic. *We must stay alive. But how?*

Breathe slowly! Diesel bows into downward dog.

I inhale long and let it out shakily. The bread pops, and Diesel barks. *Toast!*

I spread the slices with peanut butter and slam them together in a sandwich, then stuff one corner in my mouth. I break off another for Diesel.

He snaps it up. *Mmm. Better?*

My breathing slows down. I chew more slowly. Another deep breath. *A little.*

I cut the rest of the sandwich into triangles and sit them on their sides like sailboats. But the sandwich boats make me think of the beach. My heart starts knocking at my ribs. I didn't see any sailboats on that day at the lake. *Stop it*, I tell myself. *Stop imagining things.* But the images keep returning and feel so real. *Déjà vu*, or as my smart dog calls it, *déjà vécu?*

Stop it. Pat my head!

He makes me smile and that makes my heart stop knocking. *Will patting you make me feel better, or you?* I leave the food for a moment and touch his warm fur, spread my hand open, and pat him from his head down his neck.

Both. Ahhh, that is much better.

Baby Luanne joins in and hugs Diesel a little too hard.

We have a booster chair for Luanne, so I hoist her away from Diesel and into the chair. My hands shake as I buckle her straps and pass her a plastic plate with two sailboats on it. The mangled rest of the sandwich goes on a regular plate for me. I pour us each some milk, Luanne's into a sippy cup. Maybe I should save that and put it into a bottle so she can fall asleep with it. Which makes me stop again. I put the milk into a bottle that day.

Stop it! Pat me again. Diesel looks up into my eyes as my hand moves over his fur. *Trust me as I trust you.*

I swallow hard as I stroke his neck and down his rib cage. *But you shouldn't have trusted me that day.*

Love and trust always. I feel his heart pound against his rib cage. *Love and trust, love and trust.*

The swirling in my brain slows and then stops. I finish most of my sandwich, take a swallow of milk, and hear more of Diesel's thoughts.

Mmmm, crusts. So crispy and flavourful. Even though his communication with me can't be normal, his voice inside my head comforts me. It feels as though it's always been there, calming me.

I am talking inside your head to help.

While Luanne plays with her sandwich boats, I dish up some kibble for Diesel, but he gives me a mournful look. *After all I've done for you. Kibble?*

"It's good for you. It will help you stay alive longer," I tell him.

But if I can only eat kibble, why would I want to?

Oh fine! I rip off the last corner of my sandwich and pitch it in the air. Diesel snaps it up before it lands.

Thank you! Yummy.

Meanwhile, Luanne's eyes droop as her chewing slows down.

"You need a nap, baby."

Her head bobs up. "No nap." Then it nods down again. She's falling asleep in the chair, which doesn't look comfortable at all. Or safe. I have to keep everyone in my family safe.

Everyone in our pack, Diesel agrees.

"Come on. You can use my bed." I undo the booster straps and carry her all the way upstairs to my room, Diesel pushing me to the side as he leads the way. "Hey! Careful!" I yell at him.

I must go first to check for predators.

"You happy?" I ask as he circles my room.

He slumps on the floor. *Yes. All clear.*

I lower Luanne onto my bed. When her body touches the mattress, her eyes pop open again.

"No nap," she cries, her little fists hitting my chest.

"No hitting!" I grab her hands and look her in the eyes. "If you promise to stay in the stroller, we'll just walk around the yard."

"Walkies!" she burbles.

Walkies! Diesel agrees.

Going back outside in that heat — how could I suggest that? Last time through, Luanne and I stayed in Aunt Cathie's cool basement watching kids' shows on a fuzzy screen all afternoon.

But now Diesel and Luanne both stare up at me, glomming on to the idea. "All right then," I say. Luanne in my arms, we head downstairs. My goal is, of course, for the motion to lull her to sleep. I strap her into the stroller and allow Diesel to rush out the back door ahead of us to "check for predators." That way he won't bowl us over. Safer for all.

Then I lift the stroller down the steps to the patchy grass and hard dirt that is our lawn. The parched ground makes pushing Luanne around a little easier, so I walk the stroller along the fence. The first time around the yard, Luanne's head begins to nod. On the second pass, her head droops. The third pass, she slumps totally asleep.

Visitor! Visitor! Diesel barks, and Luanne's head immediately jerks up. She looks around, her eyes open wide. *Wiener Girl is here!* Diesel tells me.

"What are you, a hamster?" Morgan's voice startles me. The gate clatters shut behind her. "How many more times are you going to go around this yard?"

Friday, June 25:

The Secret

Morgan is Wiener Girl? I think. Then I try to concentrate on Morgan's question. "Well, if you hadn't woken Luanne up, I could stop circling the yard around now, thanks very much."

"And if you had a cellphone, I woulda called you."

Luanne bobs up and down in the stroller, arms reaching.

I reach down and unbuckle her. Hating how Morgan snuck up on us, I scoop up the baby and turn to face her. "What are you doing here?"

"I looked for you at your aunt's house but you weren't there." Her lips part to reveal large white teeth, her standard grin. It always seems like she has some secret joke going.

"Made me think you didn't have the brat today, but I can see I'm wrong."

"Stayed home sick." I bounce Luanne on my hip and sway.

"Shouldn't you be in bed, then?" She tilts her head and narrows her eyes. "Won't the kid catch whatever you have?"

"Heatstroke? Not contagious."

"You don't even look hot." She reaches to touch my forehead, but I bounce away. "Should you be outside, then?"

"Going in, right now."

"No, don't do that. I have something to tell you. Something important."

"What?" I snap. Then I coo at Luanne: "There, there, baby girl. Put your head down. Rest."

"Don't be so impatient. Come with me to the park."

Park, park, park, park! Diesel barks.

"Shush, Diesel!" Did he even bark out loud? "Can't leave," I answer.

"Oh, don't give me that sick line. You're fine."

"I've got the dog and Luanne."

"Bring 'em both. The guys are there playing Frisbee. Waiting for the pool to open." More of her teeth show.

"No. I can't."

Morgan raises one eyebrow.

"Diesel could get hit by a car."

"Not gonna happen. He's a smart dog."

I shake my head.

Listen to Wiener Girl. She is a smart human, Diesel tells me.

No, she's not. I have to help her with all her school work. We're staying here.

But I have learned my lesson. No running in front of cars. I need to stay alive to save you.

Morgan digs her fists into her hips. "C'mon. Stop making excuses and come with me. Otherwise Simon will have already hit the pool by the time we get there."

Will this just be a repeat of my drowning in a different way? Earlier, even? "Simon?" I shouldn't have asked.

Morgan nods happily.

Last time through I mostly hid from Morgan, crying about my dog, the whole week before the beach accident. This time I have to make it go differently. And I want to believe Morgan is the kind of friend who needs to share a secret with me. Besides, I'll have Diesel with me this time.

Only, my teeth start chattering. I tuck Luanne in close, trying to soak up her baby heat.

Morgan narrows her eyes. "What's wrong with you. You've got goosebumps. Are you really sick?"

"Yes … no. It's just that when we get there … I can't go swimming. I had this strange dream." It's the easiest way to explain it to her. The way that makes me sound the sanest.

"Don't eat cookies before you go to bed. I always have bad dreams after chocolate chip."

"You don't get it. This one felt like more than a dream. Diesel ran out in front of a car and died. And I drowned. It felt real."

"So what? You think your dreams predict what will happen? That you have some kind of second sight?"

She makes it sound totally stupid. And yet, a dream that predicts the future sounds way more reasonable than drowning and coming back to life with a lump on my head and a dog's voice talking inside it. "Anyhow, I can't watch both Luanne and Diesel at the same time."

"You can't control the dog at all!" Morgan laughs at me, like usual. "I'll walk Diesel. He'll listen to me. I was the one who trained our old dog, King."

"You had a dog?" I ask.

"Yup. Told you. Something happened to his innards. We didn't have the money for the surgery so …"

Our parents are separated; our dogs died.

"I'm sorry, Morgan. I didn't know."

"Yeah, you did. Remember that food chain project? That's when King died. You were just too mad at me to listen."

"Oh." I even remember her telling me now.

"Never mind. Just watch this." She snaps her fingers. "Sit, Diesel!" Then she raises a pointer finger, but it looks as though she clutches something in her palm.

Does she have something delicious in her hand? Diesel sits and keeps his eyes trained on her hand. *Food?*

"Good dog." She opens her palm to him.

Pizza smell. Where is it? He licks her hand madly as though it's covered in mozzarella cheese, his favourite food after toast crust and meat scraps.

"So what's your news?"

Morgan just smiles. "Tell you at the park. Just get Diesel's leash."

I dash into the house, Diesel bounding after me, grab the leash off the hook, and snap it onto his collar. He leads me back outside to Morgan and Luanne.

Morgan holds out her hand for the leash. "Give it to me."

I squeeze my hand around it. "Diesel chases buses. You have to hold on really tight."

"No worries. I can control him. I've got your back."

There it is, that line again. Morgan is a good two heads taller than I am. Most people are. Does that make her stronger?

She grabs the leash from me. "Want me to do a round in the yard as a test?"

"No, that's okay. Wait here another minute. I'll be right back."

I leave Morgan with Diesel and head inside with Luanne to change her diaper, which really wakes her up all over again. Then I lock up and we set out for the park, Luanne pointing and jabbering about a birdie in the tree.

"It's a chickadee," I tell her. She chatters and I tell her more names of things. Delaying. I don't want to beg to hear Morgan's news; I'm hoping she has to burst and spill any moment.

"You know how you're always crushing on Simon?" she starts as we hit the end of the fifth block.

"C'mon. That's just a game." I clutch my hands together. "'Oooh, Simon's so hot.' I'm just playin' along with all the other girls. He's way too old and tall for me." We cross the street. "Hold the leash tighter on the road. You're not paying enough attention."

She tugs Diesel's leash to reel him in closer. "You don't like older guys?"

"They scare me. Guys in general. But anyway, no guy in high school wants to go out with someone in middle school."

"But we're done middle school now."

"Does he even know me?"

"You must have made quite an impression."

I like the idea, and I can't help smiling. But she's messing with me, has to be, so I ignore her and talk to Luanne about every little thing she sees. "Yes, pretty, those are sunflowers." We continue down the block. A bus lumbers around the corner.

Smells bad! "Rouff, rouff!" *Beware!* The fur over Diesel's back stands on end. *Large noisemaker approaches!*

Leave it! I stop Morgan and hold on to the leash with her.

Why don't you humans attack them?

They carry us places.

"Sheesh, what is it with you? Do you have trust issues?" Morgan yanks the leash away from me. "Let *me* worry about the dog."

I do find it hard to trust Morgan. It's not even about the food chain project mess-up. Or her making fun of me. Or the fact that there's something shifty about her. "Diesel chases buses. I just don't want any accidents." The truth is I don't trust anyone. Especially with important stuff: my college fund,

Dad and Mom getting back together again, or Diesel. Most of all Diesel. I feel like I've already lost him once.

"Walk nice," she commands Diesel.

I can control myself. Do not worry. To both of their credit, Diesel trots along with his little bouncy dingo step right at Morgan's heels.

Finally, I break down and ask, "How do you know Simon likes me?"

"He told me. Even back in middle school, he thought you were a fireball." She hesitates. "Or was that a dynamo?"

She has to be lying. When would she have talked to him recently? And how can he remember me when he doesn't even know I'm alive? "A peanut?" I suggest.

"No, that's my nickname for you. Something else, I forget. But he likes you."

This is what friends do, talk about their crushes and whether they like them back. I want to believe I am that kind of friend to Morgan now. But I don't. "Simon can have any girl he wants —"

"Come on, Naomi. Imagine how popular we both would be if we started high school with boyfriends."

For one moment I allow myself to think past this awful summer. To imagine myself walking to school side by side with Morgan. In my mind, I'm as tall as she is. My shoulders are back, my head and chin held high. Girls and guys say hi as we stroll onto the school grounds. Everybody sees me; everybody knows me. I'm not a teacher-pleaser or a peanut. I have a friend. I am no longer a loner.

I am so wrapped up in this daydream, I don't pay attention to the drone of an engine growing louder.

Danger, danger. Two-wheeled noisy thing coming!

Or react to Diesel's thoughts. Morgan looks up and waves at a burly guy on a motorcycle. He and the little girl sitting behind him wave back. The explosive splutter of the Harley Davidson is so loud now that Luanne covers her ears.

"Both hands on the leash!" I yell at Morgan.

Too late. Diesel rips away from Morgan. *Attack! Attack! Two-wheeled thing threatens!* He bounds toward the bike.

"Diesel, no!" With the stroller blocking me, I can't make a dive for him. My legs and arms feel weighted, like I have to pull them through water to move. Time slows.

Morgan dashes in front of Diesel, waving her hands. "Stop!"

Wild-eyed, she bends down, snatches up the leash, then freezes.

The motorcycle rumbles forward. It's going to hit both of them.

An image flashes in front of my eyes. Diesel high in the air, a Smart Car driving away. The Smart Car dissolves, and a motorcycle takes its place. Will Diesel die by motorcycle instead? Will Morgan die with him?

Is my second sight, as Morgan calls it, crooked?

At the last possible second the motorcycle rides up onto the driveway beside them and then down the sidewalk, till it comes to a stop a few metres away.

Diesel lunges for the motorcycle. *Stay away from my pack. I will bite, bite, bite you!*

The rider shuts off the engine.

Morgan yanks Diesel back by his leash. "Sorry, Uncle Lurch. Should have held him tighter. I didn't know he liked choppers. Hi, Auntie Lynn."

Bite, bite, bite, Diesel growls.

"Quiet!" Morgan stoops down, puts her arm around Diesel, and says something into his ear.

Diesel quiets down. *You are part of Pizza Girl's pack. I accept you into ours.* His tail gives a double wag as he eyes the pair on the bike.

Pizza Girl? I thought Morgan was Wiener Girl?

She smells different today. Her last meal was pizza.

Luanne begins wailing and I take her from the stroller into my arms.

The small figure on the back gets off the bike. She's wearing a red leather jacket paired with black leather pants. "Hey, Morgan."

That girl is Auntie Lynn? I bounce Luanne and sway. "Shhh, baby, it's okay. Everyone's fine."

Lynn pulls off her helmet, and her long, bright blond hair tumbles down. I see now that she looks about Mom's age, with heavier wrinkles around her eyes and mouth.

Morgan's uncle kicks down the stand and climbs off the bike. He towers over Morgan's aunt, his long beard not even grazing the top of her head. He keeps his helmet on, but a skinny black ponytail pokes out from the back. "I usually watch better for dogs," he says and then shakes his finger. "But you should train him not to do that."

"It's her dog," Morgan says, pointing to me.

Diesel's tail thumps. *I welcome Pizza Girl's noisy, smelly pack!*

I give Morgan my laser stare. *She* is supposed to be holding him. Still, I'm not going to criticize her in front of her biker folk.

"The Dog Whisperer once trained a Jack Russell to stop going crazy around bikes. He put treats on the seat and got the dog to jump on it while it was running," Morgan's aunt says.

"Want to sit up here, boy?" Uncle Lurch asks Diesel as he pats the seat. "Do you girls have any treats for him?"

What kind of treats would I get for such a leap? Toast, wieners, pizza? Diesel wags and approaches the bike. *I do not mind sitting on the two-wheeled thing. Show me the treat.*

"No, no!" I hold up my hands. I can picture the motorcycle toppling over and killing him. Maybe I do have some kind of strange second sight. "Diesel shouldn't do that. Thanks anyway."

Diesel raises his paw. *I can shake hands instead.* He slumps. *Or lie down. Rolling over is hard, but I will try.* He sways slowly to the right and lands on his side, then on his back, his legs waving in the air.

"Get up!" I tell him and turn to Morgan. "Why don't you push the stroller and let me hold Diesel's leash?"

"No. He'll be okay with me. I'll see you at the house, Auntie Lynn."

"Just in case, could you wait till we get down the street to start your engine, please?" I ask her uncle.

I will not attack any two-wheel from Pizza Girl's pack.

"Sure," he answers. "But there *are* other bikes out there."

And other buses and trucks, skateboards and scooters. Shaking my head, I look down at Diesel. "What is wrong with you?" I scold him out loud. "You know you're not supposed to chase!"

I did not chase. I attacked. I protected. It's a dog-given right. I will always save you. He pants through a proud grin.

Auugh! I just want to run back to the house with Diesel and Luanne and hide.

"That dog is an accident waiting to happen," Morgan's aunt says.

Diesel pants as he thumps his tail.

"Nah, he's fine," Morgan says. "I'll work with him."

She thinks she can, and maybe she's right. But I know in my heart that Diesel is an accident that has already happened.

Friday, June 25:

Waiting for the Accident to Happen

Once Luanne calms down, I snap her back in her stroller and we continue on. Each car and truck that passes makes my stomach knot up so tightly that I can't even talk to Morgan anymore. Finally, we turn off the street into the park, and I sigh with relief. At least there won't be any motorcycles or buses to worry about here.

Park, park, park, park! Diesel wags his whole body.

The large maple trees shade us from the sun, making the air a little cooler. As I breathe in deeply, I feel the knots loosen.

The playground and community arena sit at the far end, beyond a soccer field. Kids with beach towels and bags are lined up in front of the arena already, waiting for the pool to open. We stroll in that direction, too.

Still thinking about Morgan's biker relatives, I ask, "Do your aunt and uncle get along well?"

Morgan snorts. "Better than my parents. He adores her. Thinks it's cute that she's so petite."

"Wow."

"She makes him feel strong. He likes to protect her."

"I'm already taller than your Aunt Lynn, aren't I?"

"Sure, a li'l bit."

Up ahead a large fountain shoots water into the air, and a breeze throws some of the spray onto our faces. Luanne giggles and I can't help laughing along. It tickles.

Diesel drags Morgan. *I am very thirsty after this long walk.*

She lets him have a drink. His tongue lapping at the water makes a happy *slap slap* sound.

My dog is alive. I do a little bouncy skip behind the stroller, sort of like Diesel's walk.

"Do you think your parents ever loved each other?" I ask Morgan. "I mean, can you imagine your mom thinking your dad was hot?"

"Gross. I don't like to think about it."

"My mom and dad did, I'm sure of it."

Against a nearby trash can, Diesel lifts his leg.

"Doesn't matter if they did or didn't," Morgan says. "They don't see anything good in each other anymore or they wouldn't have split. It's over. They'll never get back together."

"How do you know?" I ask.

"My sister and I tried everything. Left chocolates with love notes on their pillows." Morgan turns and winks at me. "They were really good ones — I wrote them myself."

"But those were lies."

"We took my brother to Grandma's so they could have romantic nights alone."

"That's a great idea. I mean, I don't have a brother but maybe I could clear out of the house."

Morgan shakes her head. "My parents always ended up fighting."

Huh! "Maybe my parents are different."

"Or you're in denial."

Diesel squats to do his business. I pull an empty plastic bread bag from my pocket and shove it at Morgan.

"Are you kidding me? I'm not touching that."

"It was worth a try." I wink at her this time. "Wait here with Luanne, then." I walk over to Diesel's pile, stoop, and scoop, not even gagging at the smell.

You wrap it up to keep it fresh, says Diesel.

I quickly drop the bag in the bin.

Then you throw it away?

Can't explain right now. I giggle as we continue on.

Ahead in the soccer field, a bunch of guys play Frisbee. I spy Simon, his T-shirt tied around his waist. Morgan says he likes me. Maybe height doesn't matter. I straighten and feel tall for a moment. On the other end of the field, his red-haired friend Tom sends the Frisbee toward him.

Watch out! Flying flat thing coming our way! Diesel barks.

Simon holds one arm high in the air, reaching for the Frisbee even as he backpedals. When the yellow disc begins its downward arc, his fingers clamp around it. Simon pauses, and Diesel's tail begins its triple wag.

"Hey, Morgan!" he calls. "Hey, Peanut! How's it going?"

My mouth goes dry. I feel short all over again.

"Fine," Morgan answers for both of us, waving and grinning. Diesel strains at the leash to pull her over to Simon. I race after with the stroller.

As we draw closer, I can't lift my eyes. If I do, I will have to see his face and speak to him. So instead I end up staring at his bare chest. This is so embarrassing.

Diesel's tail slaps against my leg. *I love this boy. Can we add him to our pack?*

No.

Morgan nudges me and I glance her way. She raises her eyebrows and nods. I know that means I'm supposed to say something.

My eyes finally lift. "How are you?"

"Great." He squats to talk to the dog. "And what's this puppy called?"

"Diesel," I answer.

He pats the dog and turns to Luanne. "Hi there, cutie. What's your name?"

Luanne just stares back at him, almost the way I do.

"This is my cousin, Luanne." Progress. I put five words together this time.

"Hey, Luanne, are you coming to play in the park?"

I like the way his eyes crinkle as he smiles.

Pat me, pat me! I love and admire you. Diesel goes crazy, slobbering over him for attention.

"Hey, Diesel. Do you like Frisbee?" Simon holds the yellow disc in front of his muzzle.

Let me sink my teeth into it. I would like that.

"Well, he loves catching stuff." The good thing about having Diesel along is people will talk to him and then I can answer for him. *Thank you, Diesel!*

I am happy to bite the yellow plate for you.

"But Diesel's not too good at bringing anything back." Having a dog makes it way easier to carry on a conversation about nothing. Especially with someone everyone crushes on.

"Wanna try?" Simon asks Diesel.

Yes, yes. Throw the dish.

"How about you, Peanut?"

Short, short. Peanut. "Nah, I've got Luanne."

"Go ahead." Morgan winks at me. "I'll watch her."

Why is she winking? She knows I'm a klutz. Does she want me to look stupid in front of Simon? "I won't be very good. Diesel can do it."

Simon curls back his hand and sends the Frisbee sailing.

I quickly unsnap Diesel's leash and he tumbles after it.

Oh yes. Oh yes. This is something at which I am skilled.

The Frisbee has a head start, and Diesel gallops a good dog's length behind. Suddenly, he leaps into the air, stretches full out, and snaps his jaws onto the rim.

Gotcha!

Morgan and Luanne cheer. Teeth clenched around the Frisbee, Diesel grins.

From the other end of the field, Tom comes running. "Wow! Let's put that dog on DogTok!" he calls. He whips out a cellphone from his back pocket. "Can you get him to do it again?"

"Only if we can get the Frisbee back!"

Just try to get your flat thing. Diesel runs to the other side of the field with the disc in his mouth. I tear after him. Another guy tries to grab it from him, but Diesel dodges away.

Simon races toward Diesel.

You can't catch me. I am too fast for you. Diesel runs away from him, cutting across the parking lot.

"Diesel, no! Not on the blacktop!"

That's when I see it. Small and bright red, like a toy. It's turning. A Smart Car.

Friday, June 25:

Training Failure

"You stupid dog. Come here!" I scream.

I run to the parking lot and dive for him. My fingers barely catch Diesel's collar as the tiny car spins around and heads back out to the road.

"Too fast!" Simon calls after the driver. "There are children playing here!"

"And dogs!" yells Morgan.

I drag Diesel to the grass again. "What were you thinking? You could have been killed!" My voice sounds too high and squeaky even to my own ears.

I caught the yellow plate. Here. Diesel spits out the Frisbee and sits up straight and tall. *I did not chase the smelly, noisy thing. I did not go into the road.*

"It's not the dog's fault," Morgan says.

"You're right." I still sound like someone about to cry. "Did anyone catch the car's licence plate number? Does anyone recognize the car or the driver?"

"What's your problem? Why do you want their licence?" Tom asks.

"That car ran over my dog!"

"What are you talking about?" Morgan squints at me. "It didn't even come close."

I shudder. My head swirls for a moment. I grip the back of it and feel the bump. *Not in this lifetime.* "I meant it could have run over Diesel. I think we should find that car. Call the police. Get them to give the driver a ticket."

"I think you're nuts," Morgan says.

"Diesel's a terrific dog. I don't blame you for wanting to report that driver," Simon says.

We should add him to our pack. Can he throw the yellow plate again?

"No, I am not letting you play!" I say out loud. I snap up the Frisbee and hold it up, out of Diesel's reach. But for him it's game on again. He leaps. High. Paws leaving the ground.

Tom trains his phone on him.

I fling the Frisbee away, over in Simon's direction. He catches it, then throws it far and high toward another player.

But Diesel takes off running and leaps again. His legs stretch full out, and it looks like he's flying. He touches down, so light and quick. It doesn't seem like he'll catch up to it, but then he takes an even longer, higher leap, twisting in the air. His teeth snatch the Frisbee.

So satisfying!

"Awesome," Simon says. "You should train that dog."

"You wouldn't have to worry about cars then," Morgan says. She pushes her hair behind her ears and grins at Simon. "I tell her that all the time!"

Right. She tells me a lot of things. I feel so out of control. I'm still shaking. I slump to the ground.

"Don't you own an extend-a-leash?" Tom asks. "When he catches the Frisbee, you can pull him back, force him to give it back to you."

Diesel sits down, tall and proud, still gripping the Frisbee between his teeth. *I am the guardian of the flat thing. I can bring it back. But you will just throw it away again.*

Simon shakes his head. "Nah, don't force the dog. Bribe him with treats instead, and he'll want to bring you the Frisbee. Hold up. I've got a piece of beef jerky in my backpack." As he strolls toward the goalpost where the backpack lies, he already has Diesel's interest. The dog prances closely at his heels.

I smell salty meat. You may have the flat thing in exchange.

When Simon unsnaps the side pocket, Diesel sits tall again, one ear up and the other down.

I start to breathe more evenly. Maybe Diesel *can* be trained to avoid cars.

I want this salty meat.

Simon bites off a tiny wedge of jerky and holds it up to his eye. "Look, boy. Diesel, look."

I can, indeed, see your salty meat.

Diesel's eyes never leave that bit of beef jerky. My hands stop shaking.

Simon gives it to him and then rips off another wedge. He pitches the Frisbee and Diesel catches it, and this time Simon puts the jerky to his eye. "Look, Diesel. Bring!"

There is more? Diesel drops the Frisbee and runs toward Simon.

"No, Diesel. Bring." Simon is patient, pointing toward the Frisbee. "Bring!"

But you keep throwing it away!

"If you want the jerky, you have to bring the Frisbee."

Silly human. Diesel bites at the Frisbee again. Then he lopes over to Simon and spits it at his feet.

I can't help smiling.

Simon exchanges a bit of jerky for the disc. With each throw and wedge of dried meat, Diesel becomes faster at returning the Frisbee.

More salty meat. More! More! More!

Maybe we *can* also train him to come when called.

Mesmerized by the antics, Luanne barely blinks. Her head nods forward a couple of times, and she jerks it up to keep watching. Finally, she dozes off, and Morgan can join in the game.

Morgan wears cut-off jeans so short that the white pockets

peek out from under the blue fray. Those shorts make her pale, skinny legs seem even longer as she stretches them to run. Her blond hair hangs in one smooth sheet that ends at her butt. That big bucktooth smile of hers looks so open and friendly. The rust flecks on her nose scream sunshine and fresh air.

Simon calls "Woot!" as she jumps up high and snags the Frisbee from the air.

My hair turns prickly with the humidity. Across the field, I notice that the lineup of kids is now moving into the building, all of them going to do something I can't: swim.

I think of jumping off the dock and suddenly feel so anxious again I want to throw up.

"Pool's open," Tom says, gathering up his gear.

Simon picks up his backpack. "You coming swimming, Peanut?"

I take a deep breath. "It's Naomi," I tell him.

"Naomi?" He smiles at me and his eyes crinkle, making me sorry my words came out so crabby. "Are you coming to the pool, too?"

"Rawf, rawf, rawf!"

"Can't. Not with the dog." I clip the leash back onto Diesel's collar.

"Too bad," Tom says. "Bet Diesel would be an excellent swimmer."

I can water jog with the best of them.

"Oh yeah!" I answer. "See ya." I turn to walk away, Diesel nicely at my heels, leaving Morgan to push Luanne in her stroller.

"Bye, Simon," Morgan says brightly.

"Will you stop?" I say under my breath.

"What, what am I doing?"

"Just keep walking!" I snap.

"Rowf!" *Alert! Fighting in the pack.*

She's not part of our pack, I think.

She should be. I know this. Trust me.

When we're far enough away, I tell her, "You don't listen to me. I didn't want Diesel to play Frisbee. That Smart Car killed Diesel!"

Morgan squints again. "You havin' heatstroke? It zipped around in the parking lot and left."

"No. Remember I told you about my dream? That is the car that ran him over."

Morgan's mouth drops open for a moment. "Okay. You had a nightmare. But Diesel loves playing Frisbee."

I stare at her. "Does what I say ever count?"

"But he needs the exercise and he's good at it."

"Just ignore me. I'm a peanut."

"This is me paying attention now. What do you want me to do?"

"I need to know where that driver lives. I have to stop the accident from happening again."

"Okay. How you gonna do that? Slash the tires? The owner will just replace them."

"I don't know. Talk to him. Maybe just get him to slow down."

"It was a dream, Naomi. Who's gonna listen to you?"

"Fine. I don't need your help."

Yes, we do! Diesel barks. *Bigger packs are stronger! We can bring down a moose!*

"Good," Morgan says. "Besides, we're training Diesel and we keep a leash on him. He's not going to get in the way of any car, smart or stupid."

As we walk, I keep scanning driveways anyway. Does that Smart Car driver even live in the neighbourhood? After a few more blocks I think out loud about the other half of my problem. "Okay, so we're training Diesel. Maybe you can help me with something else."

"Okay."

"Something different." I stop walking and tell Diesel to sit.

He wags his tail but remains standing. *I must at all times be ready!*

Then I turn to Morgan, grip her pale grey eyes with mine. "Can I really trust you?"

"I've got your back," we both say.

"I know you like to say that," I continue, "but you have to keep this a secret." I hesitate for a moment. This is huge, and once I say it out loud, there's no taking it back. "Can you teach me how to swim?"

"You're kidding me, right?" she says. She starts to push the stroller faster, hurrying toward our gate, Diesel following her and dragging me along. "All the more reason to dump the dog and head for the pool."

"Have you been listening? What part of *secret* do you not understand?"

"Simon might like teaching you," she calls back as she bumps open our gate with Luanne's stroller. "We know he likes tiny. Maybe it would make him feel big and strong, like Uncle Lurch. Maybe he likes helpless girls."

"I'm not helpless. And I don't want the cool high school girls thinking that. You've got my back, remember?" I unlock the door and let Diesel in. Then I take the stroller from Morgan.

She frowns. "Fine, no lessons in public. A bit trickier. Wait a minute! I have the perfect idea. I know where I can teach you how to swim. No one will ever have to know."

I have a feeling I'm not going to like her solution. When do I ever? But what choice do I have? Lessons at the community centre are out. Dad throwing me off some dock? Really, I have run out of options.

Saturday, June 26:

The First Swimming Lesson

The best part of Morgan's idea is that Diesel and Baby Luanne can come. No one will be around to insist Luanne wears a special swim diaper, the kind that Aunt Cathie may not have or want to buy. Diesel won't have to be tied up outside.

We're going to a pool that her uncle is looking after for the summer. According to Morgan, Lurch likes it to be used because the splashing and movement keep the chemicals stirred up so the water doesn't go green. Not sure I believe we have permission, since we're not allowed to go inside to use the bathroom.

"Ya gotta just hold it. If you pee in the pool, there's a chemical that will turn the water red around you."

"That's a myth," I tell her.

But just in case, on Saturday morning I go to the bath-room twice before Morgan arrives.

"We're going swimming, Luanne. You're going to love it!"

"Rawf!" *Me, too! I love water running! It's so refreshing.*

Even though Aunt Cathie has the day off, we're tak-ing my baby cousin because Mom and my aunt are pack-ing together. It's official: they decided on the ride to work together with Dad yesterday that we're moving in with her the first week of July. This is a whole different path from the last time through. Mom never told me about not making rent then. She was just endlessly mad at Dad.

But Mom isn't happy about moving, either. I hear her sighing as she empties cupboards — cupboards she lovingly painted white against a sunny yellow wall.

It's as if she's leaving a best friend instead of a townhouse rental. And she tossed Dad out so easily!

He should be helping, because I hear Mom and Aunt Cathie badmouthing him. Something they couldn't do if he were here. What did Morgan say about her parents? They could never see anything good in each other. Maybe Dad needs some help showing his good side. He's sweet and kind, but he sometimes doesn't know when and how to pitch in.

"Sure, it's great for James to live with his brother. Neither of them lifts a finger to clean up and neither of them minds," Mom says.

"One less thing to worry about. That's all men want," Aunt Cathie agrees.

Aunt Cathie seems happier about the move. She won't be alone so much. Uncle Greg only comes home once a month from Fort McMurray. Luanne will have more people around to watch her. Paying half her rent will help Aunt Cathie, too; maybe I'll finally get my babysitting money. Diesel may be right about a bigger pack being stronger. This could be the best thing all around.

I sneak off and call Dad to come over. "Mom needs you. She hates moving."

"I can't come right now, Naomi. I picked up a shift. You know I shorted her on rent money."

"Soon, then, Dad?"

"Sure. Meanwhile, I'll see you later."

Someone pounds on the side door, distracting me.

"Rawf, rawf!" *Pizza Girl has arrived.*

"Okay. Bye, Dad. Love you."

"Love you, too, Naomi."

I let Morgan in.

"Hey, Morgan. Can we stop at the grocery store before we head for the pool? I want to buy some beef jerky," I tell her.

Salty meat! Diesel wags his whole back end.

"Why? That stuff's awful and costs a lot, too."

"Because I want to keep training Diesel."

"Simon gets that stuff for free 'cause his dad works at Willow Farms. Do you have any wieners? We can use them instead."

Wieners? I like the way Pizza Girl thinks.

Mom overhears and opens the fridge, tossing me a bag. "Here, take these. They're past their best-before date anyway."

"They won't make him sick?" I ask.

Smells delicious. I'm not fussy. Aged wiener is more flavourful. Sitting on his haunches in front of me, Diesel shifts from one front paw to the other.

"He's a dog," Morgan says. "They love rotten meat. Nuke them for minute." She takes the bag from me. "The animal shelter does this for their dog snacks. They showed me when we picked up King."

Mmm. Warm wiener, even better. Diesel's jaw drops open into a drooly pant.

The microwave dings and I use an oven mitt to remove the plate. The wieners steam and look overcooked and rubbery. But they smell good.

While they cool, I change Luanne's diaper, put her in the stroller, and make sure I have towels for both of us. Then Morgan helps me chop the wieners into thin slices, which we sweep into a plastic zip bag.

"Arouff!" *Come on! The meat smells perfect now. It does not need wrapping.*

Morgan takes Diesel's paw and makes him shake before she allows him one. In another moment she has Diesel sitting pretty, waving one paw desperately in the air.

I do all this to make you happy. Now give me more. Please!

She gives him another slice as I snap the leash on and another as we head out the door. She grabs the leash from my hand.

I push the stroller up and over the doorstep.

The morning feels cooler than the past few days, different from Saturday last time around, which I spent in the basement, trying to stay cool, reading *A Dog's Purpose* and crying. It's still warm enough to enjoy the water, but a big relief from the previous weeks. If the temperature can change, maybe life will, too.

My eyes scan all the driveways as we pass. No Smart Car there, none there, nope, and nope. It has to belong somewhere. It's probably on the road now. I tense up and glance at my watch, hoping the numbers have changed. But it flashes *THU July 01 4:30.*

When we are safe, the time counter will begin again, Diesel reminds me.

We're going swimming — what could be more dangerous? My pulse pounds hard in my ears like the surf at the ocean. My breathing gets quicker.

After each block that Diesel walks close to Morgan's heels, we stop, get him to sit, and then allow him a sliver of cooked wiener.

This slows us down. You should just give me all the meat, Diesel says.

You need to learn not to run into the street.

He answers with a whining single note.

And he's right. It's taking forever. And where is that Smart Car? I tense up whenever a skateboarder rattles by or we pass a bus stop, all the sounds and sights that set Diesel off usually. I watch Morgan, hoping she's holding the leash tight enough.

Without the dog, we might have taken the bus because this house is all the way over in the university part of the town. Morgan tells me a professor lives there during the school year. A professor writing on the impact of biker traffic. "And he trusts a biker to look after his pool?"

"Well, yeah! Even rock stars hire bikers for security. No one messes with them. Here we are. Isn't this worth it?"

The tall grey stone building looks like a castle. What I wouldn't give to live in a house like this. I sigh. "Wow. Maybe."

As we make our way through the black iron gate at the side, I can see the backyard looks posh, too. A patio made of grey and beige slabs extends from the door and surrounds the kidney-shaped pool. A cedar-shingled hut stands near the corner. Along the sides, ferns and grasses grow in a stone trough. The lawn between the trough and the fence looks spring green, so bright I can't believe it lived through the same heat as the rest of the city.

I love this soft grass. Diesel barks as he lifts his leg against the fence.

Morgan shimmies out of her shorts and peels off her top. Then she runs to the other end of the pool. "Check this out!" She turns a tap at the back of a rocky wall and water tumbles over it. "Our own waterfall!"

Diesel paces, barking and leaping to snap his jaws at the little falls. *There is wild white water here. Danger!*

Relax. It won't hurt us.

He keeps pacing anyway.

Meanwhile, I strip Luanne down to her diaper. Then I pull a pair of rubber pants over it and put an old T-shirt on her to protect her from the sun.

"Don't you have any water wings for her?" Morgan asks.

I shake my head.

"So you gonna change or what?"

I pull off my T-shirt and shorts.

She stares at my pink one-piece. "That is one ugly bathing suit."

I shrug. "It was a birthday present from my aunt a few years ago."

"Little Mermaid almost makes sense when you're ten." She squints at my butt. "And it still fits?"

"Sad, right? I don't go swimming much anyway, seeing as I don't know how."

"Yeah, well, the back's worn clean through." She shakes her head and turns to Luanne. "Come on, brat." Luanne doesn't seem to mind her new nickname. Morgan reaches for her hand and, smiling, Luanne takes it. Together they step down the stairs into the water.

I follow more slowly. Ahh! Perfect. If only I could learn to float on top of it.

Morgan dips Luanne down into the pool with her. Together they drift away from the edge.

Diesel runs back and forth nervously. *Careful, careful!*

"Okay. So show me what you can do," Morgan says to me. "Try to swim to that side." She points to the other side of the shallow end.

"I can't get that far."

"Try." Meanwhile, she crouches down in the water near me, with Luanne gurgling and splashing.

I sink down and then run in the water, the way I learned in my single swimming lesson.

"You're just treading water," Morgan says.

Not even. I sputter as I sink.

"Stop, stop!" Morgan holds out her hand, and I death-grip it. "I know you have no coordination at all, but can you close your mouth when you swim?"

"Can you stop being so mean?" I snap.

"What? Did I say something we all don't know?"

"I can't help it — I'm a klutz. Just like you're a dolt and can't help that!"

Anger! Diesel barks loud and sharp at us. *Fighting in the pack!* I remember him barking like that when Mom and Dad fought.

"Quiet, Diesel!" He makes me regret yelling at Morgan.

"I am dumb." Morgan shrugs.

I sigh. "Since we both agree we're clumsy and stupid, can we stop telling each other? It's bad for our self-esteem!"

Morgan snorts at that, which makes me crack up, too. Baby Luanne laughs along with us, happy to share a chuckle. Diesel stops barking and runs to the waterfall again.

"What I meant was," Morgan explains, "it may be hard to move your hands and feet at the same time, but concentrate on closing your lips. You don't want to swallow water." She begins blowing bubbles with Luanne.

I blow along with them.

"See, when you blow bubbles, you're pushing air out so the water can't come in to your mouth. It's the first thing they teach babies when they're learning to swim."

"I'm not a baby!"

"I never said you were. Sheesh. I just meant it was an easy baby step." She shakes her head. "Instead of standing straight up in the water, try leaning forward and make your hands run, too, like a dog."

Mouth closed is not all that easy. I have to focus on breathing through my nose. But when both my feet and hands churn, I move forward a little before I sink.

Careful! Diesel leaps into the water and swims over. *Look at me. Watch my paws.*

"I can't believe he did that," Morgan says. "It's like he wanted to show you how." She shakes her head.

"Or save me." *I'm fine*, I tell him with my thoughts and guide him over to the stairs. I don't want him to drown while I figure out swimming. He scrambles out and shakes himself.

"Okay, let's try something different. The dog-paddle is too much work," Morgan says. "How about the breaststroke? Way easier. Here's what I want you to do." She sits Luanne on the edge of the pool and puts her own hands together, prayer-style, at the top of her chest. Then she pushes out and opens her arms. Luanne reaches her arms out, mimicking her. "Don't even bother with your legs right now. Just scrunch down and practise the move. No, no! Push the water away with your palms!"

Luanne leans over.

"Watch out!" I call.

Morgan turns. Too late — Luanne face-plants into the pool.

"Woof!" *I must save the human pup!* Diesel jumps in.

Morgan ducks down after the baby. The water pushes against my legs as I run toward them. Too slow! I've heard how quickly little kids can drown.

Like with my watch, time stops. The world quits turning. What's taking Morgan so long?

I run with the force of my drowning memory pushing against me. A picture flashes across my mind, Baby Luanne blue-faced at the bottom of the pool.

Diesel thrashes madly toward them.

This is taking too long. Has Morgan knocked her head on the bottom? What about Luanne's heart? Can she take this kind of scare?

I can't swim. I can't save them. My heart pounds.

Finally their heads reappear. Luanne blinks hard and coughs. Diesel, of course, barks.

We're okay!

Luanne starts to cry.

Morgan pats Luanne's back. "There, there," she says stiffly. "You're fine."

"We have to go home," I say. Diesel and I climb up the pool stairs together.

"Oh, come on," Morgan calls. "Luanne was under the water for like two seconds."

Was it really only a couple of seconds?

Time counting stops. Diesel's thoughts.

What does that even mean? I wonder.

Until we're safe, he repeats.

All of us, even Luanne? I ask.

Our pack. Everyone.

I snap, "She could have died, Morgan!"

"Shhh! Stop!" Morgan's eyebrows push together and she gives me a look. Then she softens her voice. "You just had a little scare, right, Luanne? That should teach you better than to jump in."

"It should teach *you*!" I'm overreacting, I know it. I was just so sure Luanne was drowning. My heart hammers. I have to keep her safe. "You can't turn your back on a baby near a pool."

The human pup is safe. Calm, calm. Drool with me. Diesel pants a huge string of dribble.

"Okay, okay. I'm sorry. I won't." Morgan sighs. "Water wings, I'm telling you. Let's just keep going."

"I have to go pee."

"Didn't you go before we left?" Morgan complains.

"Yes, but Luanne falling in scared me. I always have to go when I'm tense."

"Fine. Go behind the pool house."

"Maybe there's a key to the pool house under a rock somewhere." I start searching.

"Forget about it. And we're not taking off yet."

I shake my head, hating the idea. But I *have* to learn how to swim, and I'm always going to be anxious near water. We'll never get anywhere if we quit whenever I get nervous. Step one means conquering my nerves. I climb out of the water and walk behind the little cedar house. Diesel circles me, barking his head off.

"Shh, boy, shh!"

Small four-leggeds are tunnelling in this ground! He starts digging madly at a hole under the fence, dirt flying. I can't afford to care right now. I need him to be quiet, and the dirt throwing gives him something to do. *I must get to them.* Tongue hanging to the side, he pants silently as I crouch down low, making myself even smaller than usual. Here in this fancy neighbourhood, surrounded by trees and a wrought iron fence, I pull the crotch of my bathing suit to the side.

Finished, I pull Diesel away from his digging and manage to replace the sod he dislodged. I stomp on it. No one will ever know what either of us has done.

That's when I sense I'm being watched. I turn, nothing. Something makes me look up, and there, at the open window of the house next door, I spy a wrinkled apple face squinting at me.

Saturday, June 26:

Gathering New Pack Members

"I see you back there. Up to no good." The white-haired woman shakes her fist at me. "I'm going to call the police!"

Angry elder! Diesel barks.

I don't answer either of them, just scoot around the pool house back to Morgan. Diesel follows at my heels. "Quick, let's go," I tell her. "The neighbour spotted me as I was going to the bathroom."

"I heard. Don't worry. Uncle Lurch told me about the old lady. No one ever listens to her. She always" — Morgan raises two fingers of each hand to make air quotes — "'calls the police.'"

I look back. The apple face disappears from the window. "You don't think she'll do it?"

"Who cares? We're allowed to swim here. Uncle Lurch said."

"But I peed on the grass!"

"C'mon. Guys do it all the time." Morgan grins. "Come back here. I want you to try a different move now. Hold on to the edge of the pool and kick your legs like a frog."

I look toward the window again. Someone closes it, then the blinds.

"Forget about her. Her caretaker probably took her away."

Maybe Morgan's right. I'm overreacting to everything these days. We're not safe until my time counter moves again, after all. I step back down into the pool, clinging to the edge as I shuffle along the side into the deeper water. I feel like an idiot. Why couldn't I have learned all this when I was four?

You're doing great! From the pool deck, Diesel leans toward me and washes my face with his tongue.

Morgan guides Luanne around the shallow part of the pool by her forearms, churning them as they go. "Big arms, and kick, kick, kick."

Luanne looks happy and excited, her near-death experience forgotten. If only I could be like her. Diesel watches from the side, one ear up, the other folded down.

"She's going to learn before you do," Morgan says.

"You're being mean again!" But she's also telling the truth, which is the way it always goes with her jabs.

My arms and legs never quite work together.

Baby Luanne turns whiny. If we were home, I would give her a bottle or a snack. That's when I realize the gnawing at my stomach isn't just nerves. "Hey, I'm starving. Let's go."

Yes, yes. Food, food. Diesel circles.

"Probably as far as we're going to get today anyway. I'm hungry, too." Morgan lifts Luanne out of the water and up onto the patio. She hoists herself out and, to her credit, moves Luanne farther away from the pool.

As Morgan dries herself off, I pull my shorts and top on over my wet suit. There's no changing room anywhere. Dark patches appear instantly all over my clothes. Then I put a dry diaper on Luanne and dress her back in her outfit.

"Hold up the towel for me," Morgan tells me, with her back to the pool house.

I raise my Cheerios cereal towel, so old and threadbare anyone can probably see through it, as Morgan strips off her two-piece. She reaches in her backpack and puts on dry underwear. Then her clothes.

What do the wet patches on my butt and crotch matter? We're going straight home anyway. The damp will keep me cool.

From the corner of my eye, I notice Diesel chewing at something. "What have you got in your mouth?" I ask and drop my towel so I can grab him to check.

The treat meat. You said it was old anyway. Why do you want to save it? He dodges away, teeth clenched over the treat bag.

"He stole the wiener bits from my pocket," Morgan calls.

It is past time to eat, Diesel says.

Most dogs only eat twice a day.

Diesel runs for the waterfall side of the pool, leaving a trail of wiener slices behind him. I scoop them up and chase after him.

Run, my pack, run!

"Don't eat the plastic!" I beg Diesel.

This is fun. Catch me!

Dodging from one side to the other, I finally corner him and make a lucky grab for the bag. It tears completely, but there is nothing much left in it anyway. Dragging him by the collar back to the gate, I snatch up all the spilled bits of wiener so he can't get those.

"Bad dog!" Morgan scolds, something I might have done, too, a lifetime ago.

"Don't call him that!" Things are different since I woke up with that lump on my head. I know why Diesel does things. I know it's not his fault. "He's just hungry like us." I raise one pointer finger in front of his face and he instantly sits. "Good dog!" I offer him a slice of wiener.

He snaps it up. *Of course I am a good dog. I am the best of good dogs.*

I pat him while Morgan hitches his leash to him again. Then we head back for home, me checking driveways. No Smart Car anywhere. Which means it's driving the streets somewhere.

Traffic grows heavier, and I hope the few slivers of wiener we have left will keep Diesel behaving.

Still a couple blocks from home, he begins barking and straining at the leash. *People are coming!*

"What's wrong with you?" Morgan asks.

I smell the boys with the dish. His bark is the only thing that sounds outside my head. "Rowf!"

Luanne starts bobbing up and down in the stroller.

Sure enough, Simon and Tom are near the end of the block, heading toward us.

"Hi, girls!" Simon calls. Tom waves.

As they draw closer, Diesel bucks like a stallion. *Hurray! It is Salty Meat Boy!*

"Down," Morgan tells him, pushing his head.

I must show my affection for him.

Simon stands in front of Diesel. "That's okay, Diesel," he coos. "When you sit calmly, I'll pat you."

I like you, I like you. Why don't you like me back? As Diesel jumps on his leg, Simon butts him down with his knee.

"He's getting better. Honestly, he is," I tell Simon. Or am I just hoping? But as if on cue, Morgan lures Diesel into a sit with a slice of wiener.

Simon looks up from Diesel and smiles. His eyes meet mine and my legs turn into noodles. Then he lowers his gaze to my chest.

I look down at the splotch of wet down my front

"She didn't pee herself, if that's what you're thinking," Morgan pipes in. "I know 'cause she did that in the yard."

I punch her arm.

"Ow!"

No hitting! Diesel barks. *Bad, bad, bad, bad!*

"I never thought that," Simon answers, chuckling.

Tom grins like a fool. He's been staring, too. "You girls going to the pool this afternoon?"

"Yes," Morgan answers.

"No," I say at the same time.

We turn to each other and she gives me a look: skinny-eyed, tight-lipped.

"I can't go. I'm seeing my father," I explain. Last time through this week, Mom cancelled Dad's weekend for me. Told him I was just too "overwrought" to go. Because of Diesel. So I really want to visit with Dad this time around. I wouldn't go to the pool anyway. There's too many people and I still can't swim. I could drown.

"Well, I'll be at the pool," Morgan says, hand on her hip. She gives me a wink.

I want to shake her for showing me up like that. And how can you trust someone who keeps winking at you?

After we say goodbye to the boys I give her the silent treatment. Luanne falls asleep as we turn onto the last block home.

Diesel growls. *Friendly, be friendly.*

"You don't have to be mad at me, Naomi. It's good I'm going. I'll keep track of Simon for you. Did you see the way Tom was looking at me?"

"No, I didn't see that. I saw him staring at the wet spots on my shirt."

"Wouldn't it be great? You get Simon and I get Tom. High school is looking better and better."

"Did you have to tell them about me going to the bathroom in the yard?"

"Arrooowh!" Diesel howls. *Tone of voice. We need more pack members.*

"Better than them thinking you'd gone in your pants. Honestly, I try to do nice things for you —"

"Do you, actually? I'm never sure."

"I just spent a couple of hours trying to teach you how to swim. Here I am letting your T. Rex lead me around."

She is being nice about that, I have to admit. But I can't help wondering, is there something she hopes to get out of all this?

Finally at the house, we let Diesel in ahead of us and then carry the stroller in with Luanne still asleep.

Morgan hangs around as though she expects something more.

"Thanks, Morgan. I do appreciate you helping with my swimming."

"Your dad really coming then?" she asks. "I thought that was just a line. 'Cause we can do something else. We don't have to go to the pool."

"Nope, it's my weekend with Dad." I stop and look at her. Could it be that she really wants me as a friend? "Unless he cancels 'cause he has to work."

She grins. "Yeah, they do that a lot, don't they?"

"Not my dad. He never gets enough hours." Still, Morgan and I are not so different anymore. We live in the same crappy neighbourhood and both have split-up parents. We're like one dog away from being identical twins.

But my parents don't have to stay apart. If something happens to me, they will need each other. Besides, I know I can help them get back together. They just need that romantic date. The one that didn't work for Morgan's parents. "Morgan, do you think I could come for a sleepover sometime soon? I've never been."

"Never? Sure. When do you get back from your dad's?"

"Sunday. But give me a day to get my stuff together." I need the time to sort out Dad, really, get him and Mom to set up that date. "Can I come, say, Tuesday?"

"Sure. Mom will be okay with that. Not a school night, after all."

She shrugs and then waits for a moment, like she wants to go with me. But I can't invite her along when I finally have Dad to myself. There are things I need to discuss with him. I can give him a few pointers on winning Mom back. Talk him into that Tuesday-night date. Not like I can do that with her big mouth around.

"Well, I'll be going." Her smile fades and she looks lost.

"See you. Have fun at the pool."

"Won't be the same without you." She heads out the door.

"Morgan?" I call after her.

"Rouff," Diesel calls.

"Yeah?"

"Can you teach me some more on Monday?"

"Sure." She grins, and for a few seconds I think, *Wow, she is turning into a real friend.* Then she continues. "I'll bring my brother's old water wings for Luanne." She winks. "And his potty for you."

And then I just want to shake her all over again.

Saturday, June 26:

Dad's Weekend

On the drive to Uncle Leo's house, where Dad has lived since the anniversary disaster, Diesel stands on my lap, mashing his body against me and squeezing me into the car door. I double-check that it's locked.

We are moving very fast. I must be near the escape hole.

"It's okay, boy. Here, let me open the window for you." I roll it down. *Just don't jump out.* I hold on to his body just in case. None of us will be safe till the time on my watch moves again.

The wind blows some of his drool back onto my arm. Dog relaxation. *I smell lake and fish!*

Diesel's thoughts remind me about my drowning. I turn to Dad. "Whatever happened to those swimming lessons you promised me this summer?" If he can teach me, too, maybe I can learn faster.

"Sorry I've been so busy. Tomorrow afternoon. We'll start then. For sure tomorrow."

"Great. You know Mom's working really hard to pack up everything for the move?"

"For sure. Your mother never lets up. Sometimes I'd just like to see her relax a bit and enjoy herself."

"Honestly, I think she needs you for that."

"I thought she'd love being able to watch movies on a big screen. Like having a date right inside the house."

"Dad, she was just cranky from the heat." The last time through this weekend, when I stayed home with Mom instead of vising Dad, all we did was watch movies. She loved it. I don't think she really ever wanted me to go off with Dad. "Why don't you borrow a movie from the library one night and surprise her?"

"I've tried and tried with her till I just don't know what to do."

I sigh. "Tuesday I'm going to a sleepover at Morgan's. Tuesday night would be good."

Dad doesn't say anything for a moment. "They have *Apocalypse* at the library. We haven't seen that one yet."

"Noooo! Something romantic!"

"Hmm. An end of the world story, I thought that was kinda romantic." Dad scratches his head.

"Ask the librarian for help. They must have a list of top tens." Something's happening with Diesel and it's distracting me. Through my forearms I feel a vibration, a rumble even, rippling across his sides and stomach. Then there's a sound like a sputter coming from his butt.

Dad waves his hand in front of his face. "Pew, what have you been feeding that dog?"

"Wieners." I open my window wider and cling tighter.

I am ready for more food now. Diesel's toenails dig into my thighs as he suddenly shifts, jerking forward. "Rouff, rouff!" *Alert! I can smell a long-eared thing out there somewhere.*

"Leave it, Diesel!" I tell him in a soft voice. "Live and let live."

He sneezes, turns toward me, and licks my face — *I love you, love you* — till I finally have to push him away. Still, I'm smiling, and if it works on me, it could work on Mom. I turn to Dad. "You could try telling Mom you love her."

"You think that would do it?" He continues to watch the road ahead.

"It might. Plus you told me you would help Mom pack."

"The way she helped me?" He grins. Grinning is good — means he isn't angry about it anymore.

"I don't think so." I remember how Mom flung his suitcase out the door because of the egg experiments. "Wait a minute. Did you see that sign?"

"What sign?"

I turn around. "That one!" I point. "It says *SCHOOL BUS DRIVERS NEEDED. FREE TRAINING.*"

"That's been up forever. I don't even notice it anymore."

"Well, you could check into it."

He reaches over and ruffles my hair. "What makes you think I haven't already?" He's smiling again. Something's up.

Everything lifts inside me. "What aren't you telling me?"

"Just finished my training. It's why I've been so busy lately. Between the classes and driving practice —"

"Dad, that's amazing! Why didn't you tell Mom?"

"I was afraid I might not pass. I still have to do the Saint John's Ambulance course this week. But when school starts, I should be driving. It's only another part-time job. She won't be impressed."

"I think she will." I smile back at Dad, lifting a hand to high-five with him. His hand meets mine.

Once we arrive at Uncle Leo's, the celebration continues. Uncle Leo sets up his portable fireplace in the backyard. Yay!

Even before the drought, outdoor fires were banned in our city and Mom sure wouldn't let Dad start one. But here we are now, picking up dead branches that the last windstorm blew from the trees.

Even Diesel helps. *Sticks, so many sticks. I love chewing sticks.*

In exchange for a treat, he occasionally drops them near the fireplace.

When we've collected a stack, Dad crumples a section of old newspaper, piles on some of the twigs, and adds a squirt of lighter fluid to the mix. Leo throws a match in and a magic pop bursts open into orange flames.

"Rawf!" Diesel leaps back.

Dad hands me a stick and a wiener. "Fresh from the Willow Farms outlet."

Diesel, eyeing the wiener, draws closer again.

"You applied there, too?" The smile on his face is all the answer I need. "Seriously? You should tell Mom."

"Nah. I left my resumé, that's all. What if nothing comes of it? I can't keep doing that to her."

"But she needs to know you're trying. She needs to hope things will get better again." I turn my stick over the flames and smell the rawhide aroma of the wiener cooking, see the skin bubble up.

"Your mother should know that about me. She should have faith."

"I don't know, Dad."

"Now don't you go blabbing to her. I'll tell her about the bus driving in my own good time."

"Those dogs look about done," Uncle Leo interrupts.

Diesel sits next to me, both ears up. *Mmmm. Smells good!*

"Did you make a salad?" I ask. "You know Mom likes us to have vegetables."

"What do you call this?" Uncle Leo bangs a relish jar down on the patio table. "All kinds of green things mushed together. And this." He sets down a ketchup bottle beside it. "A tomato salad, only you don't have to chew."

"I could get cheese and bacon. We could make whistle dogs," Dad suggests.

"You're funny, Dad. Uncle Leo's closer with his ketchup and relish."

"Okay, I'll serve something more healthy." Dad runs back into the house and brings out pickles. "And we have sauerkraut."

"I can heat up some beans," Uncle Leo says.

I roll my eyes. With Mom, our plates are mostly filled with vegetables. With Dad and Uncle Leo, it's junk food every day. We eat on those cheap paper plates that the chip stands use so there are no dishes, except for some knives and forks.

Uncle Leo drops a wiener in the ashes but he pokes it back out and gives it to Diesel. *Why, thank you!* Happiness all around.

After the wieners, we roast marshmallows. Dad likes to set his on fire and watch them flambé. "Tell me this isn't the best," he says as he holds it out for me to sample.

The crispy outside tastes bitter, which contrasts nicely with the melted extra-sweet inside, opposites working together deliciously. It hits me like a punch in the stomach. Dad and Mom are like that, too: opposites that could work to bring out the best in each other — Dad fun and carefree, Mom hard-working and responsible. They could be an awesome combo. Instead, it's like their marshmallow is so burnt, it's falling off the stick into the fire.

After supper, we don't clean up much. Uncle Leo tosses everything in a big garbage bag that he throws in his shed. Diesel scores one of our plates — *Chewy round disc* — and shreds it under the table as Dad brings out sleeping bags and we open up the deck chairs. Uncle Leo sets up his little TV so we can watch the baseball game. "Just like at the drive-in," he comments.

"Yep." It's never dark enough for the first movie at the drive-in, either. I just lie back and listen to the ball game. The pale picture isn't a big deal to Uncle Leo, since his set is a junk-day find. The screen image looks snowy at any time of day, inside the house or out. As the innings play on, the sky glows orange and pink till the sun sinks, leaving a golden glow on the outlines of the houses.

The Blue Jays are losing to the Yankees, so it's easy to drift off to sleep.

My eyes grow heavy as the sky darkens. Summer's rushing by. My summer, my life … muddled, sleepy thoughts.

Pinprick stars wink in the sky. I search for Sirius, the Dog Star. Not out. It hides behind the sun. I reach down to pat Diesel, curl my fingers in his fur.

Will our family rise up again, or is it all just burnt marshmallows? I sigh.

I will save you. I will save our pack.

Stay safe yourself, I think, and fall asleep.

• • •

Alert! Alert! Alert! Diesel's bark, loud and shrill, wakes me. The motion sensor lights flash on. *We are under attack. I must defend us!* I spin around in the chair to see him backing a black-and-white creature toward the shed. First I think he's cornered a cat because it's hissing.

"Leave it!" I yell at him. When I squint I realize it's a skunk. Aren't skunks supposed to be timid? This one stomps his feet and charges forward. Maybe he has rabies.

"No, Diesel!" Instead of a Smart Car throwing him in the air, will a rabid skunk bite him and kill him? I struggle out of my sleeping bag and run to grab him.

Too late. I worried about the wrong thing anyway. I dodge away as the skunk flips around and raises its plume-like tail high in the air.

"Diesel!" The worst smell ever blasts into the air, sharp and a hundred times worse than dog fart.

Dad and Uncle Leo wake up and start gagging.

The skunk stalks off into the dark.

Diesel yowls. Then he lowers his head to the ground, rubbing his paws over it, rubbing his whole body desperately against the grass.

"Oh, man, that is awful," Dad says as he puts his fist to his nose and mouth.

"Diesel's been sprayed by a skunk," I explain.

"No kidding!"

"We need the hose," Uncle Leo exclaims, and he rushes to the wheel attached to the house. He turns the tap on and uncoils the long green rubber hose as Dad catches Diesel by the collar and drags him over.

But I am a good dog! Diesel yelps in protest. *I defended you.*

"It's all right, Diesel. We need to get rid of that smell." I turn to Uncle Leo. "You're supposed to use tomato juice," I tell him.

"Don't have any," Uncle Leo says. "Just grab the ketchup from the patio table."

Diesel tries to pull his head out of his collar to get away. *Don't want that water rushing at me!* Dad flings his arm around Diesel's back to hold him, wincing at the smell.

I dash over. A thick yellow comma of guck clings to the white patch on Diesel's chest. "Uncle Leo, aim the water here." He turns the hose up full blast, and when it hits poor Diesel, the water sprays Dad and me, too.

Cold hard wet hurting me!

"Turn the pressure down!" I yell.

"Try the ketchup now." Uncle Leo diverts the water with a finger.

I squirt the tomato gunk on Diesel's neck, aiming for that yellow comma.

He whimpers.

"Massage it in, Naomi," Dad tells me, still struggling to hold the dog.

I rub and scrub while Uncle Leo sprays and rinses. As the water hits Diesel's fur, a smell wafts up — rotten tomato, burnt rubber, roasted cough syrup all combined. It grows stronger.

"That wasn't enough ketchup. I'll get my spaghetti sauce," Uncle Leo says. He runs into the house and comes back with a couple of cans, garlic and hot pepper, both open and ready. Diesel licks at one. *Tangy.*

"Stop that." I grab the can. Before he can dodge, I throw the contents toward his chest, but he ducks and the sauce lands on his head.

I see red! It stings.

"Sorry, boy!" I wipe away the sauce from his eyes and try to shampoo it into his neck. Meanwhile he licks it off my hands.

Dad empties another can on his back. Together we rub it all over him. He looks like a bad accident and reeks of charred lasagna.

"Get rid of that collar," Uncle Leo says.

I unbuckle it and throw it toward the shed.

I'm wet, so wet! I want to run all over.

"Stay, Diesel." I grab at the scruff at his neck.

"There. Not so bad now," Uncle Leo says.

"You're just getting used to it." I breathe through my mouth so I don't gag.

"Smells like an all-dressed burger," Dad says. He yawns.

Uncle Leo shuts off the tap and hands me some rags. "Here. Dry him off."

I rub gently at Diesel, but his milk-chocolate fur holds a rosy hue, and the white spots on his chest and foot are pink. The bitter skunk smell surrounds me. My fingers smell like skunk now, too.

Thank you, Naomi. Diesel licks my face.

"Let's go inside," Leo says. "Not him, though." He points at Diesel.

"What, you gonna let him tangle with that skunk a second time? Uh-uh." Dad shakes his head. "C'mon, boy.

We'll set you up in the basement." He drags Diesel inside and down the stairs.

All alone. "Arooo!"

Diesel continues to howl as I bunk down on the couch in the living room. I stuff a pillow over my head so I don't hear him crying, but I can't shut out his thoughts.

I'm so alone. "Arooo!"

It's cold down here!

Come visit me, please! "Arooo!"

"Poor puppy." The entire house reeks of him anyway. My dad and uncle and me, too. I grab all the couch pillows and head downstairs to sleep with him.

How wonderful, you're here! I missed you so much! Diesel wags his whole body as I arrange my pillows on the floor near him.

Yuck! The skunk scent still scalds my nostrils. My eyes water. "I don't know if I can take it, Diesel." I wander to the washer, find a dishcloth in a laundry basket, and tie it across my nose like a mask.

"Better."

I lie down on the cushions and Diesel does a few circles on the towel bed Uncle Leo made him, finally slumping down. I sigh again. I think about what Mom would say if she were here.

She would blame this all on Dad. The illegal fire and not cleaning up all the food scraps and that huge bag of garbage stuffed into the shed — Mom would probably be right. Dad and Uncle Leo are two laid-back marshmallows. Lazy, Mom would call them.

But they are fun. Cooking and sleeping outside was great. Even the skunk thing was kind of a hoot. When that skunk turned around and blasted Diesel and the look on Dad's and Uncle Leo's faces as they woke up to that smell — all too funny.

I drape my arm over Diesel and his heartbeat lulls me to sleep.

12

Sunday, June 27:

Bleach Bath

Sunday morning, when everyone finally rolls out of bed, Dad makes pancakes with chocolate chips. I pile on the syrup and enjoy the sugar buzz. Dad forgot to buy dog food, so after I pick out the chocolate, Diesel gets the last pancake.

He downs it in two bites. *Good. Sweet.* He licks his chops. *More?*

I shake my head. *Sorry.*

Dad washes and I dry the dishes until he picks up a call.

"Yeah, hello.… This afternoon?" Dad looks at me and shrugs. "Sure, I can come in." He clicks off.

"But you promised you'd teach me to swim today!"

"We have all summer."

"No, we don't! Dad, I need to know how to swim by Canada Day."

"Come on, Naomi. What's so special about July first? With the bus driver training taking so much time, I need to pull all the extra shifts I can to pay your mom."

I could drown this Thursday. My lip buckles, but I don't tell him. I finish drying the last fork and toss it in the cutlery drawer. Somehow I knew Dad would never teach me. Instead, he borrows money from me to fill up the gas tank and then drives me and Diesel straight home.

Apart from the pink spots on the dog, the skunk adventure seems over, the smell blending with the everyday air.

Not for Mom, though.

As Diesel runs into the house, Mom yells, "Good god. Where has that dog been!" Her eyes tear and she grabs for a tissue from the box on the counter. "You don't smell so good, either."

"A skunk got him."

"And your father didn't give him a bath?"

"Of course he did. With all kinds of tomato sauce, too. You should have smelled him before."

"Well, we're going to have to wash him right this time."

No! Diesel whimpers. Then he tears off toward my room, toenails scrabbling against the floor. *Clunk!* I presume he's made a direct dive under the bed.

Mom picks up the phone. For a second I think she'll dial Dad and blast him over all this. But she says, "I'm calling the animal shelter. They'll know what to do."

If she'd let Dad hook us up to the internet, we could just look it up.

Because it's Sunday, it takes her a few moments to get through to an emergency attendant. Then she jots down some notes and puts her hand over the receiver. "Naomi, can you get the hydrogen peroxide, please?"

I look around at all the boxes she and Aunt Cathie packed already, wondering where it could be.

"On the top shelf of the medicine cupboard. We left that stuff for last."

By the time I find it, she's started filling a pail from the tub faucet. The water bubbles up. "Dishwashing liquid," she explains to me. "Now baking soda." She shakes some in. "Pour in the peroxide. That should be about right." The whole thing fizzes like a chemistry experiment. "We have to shampoo this all over Diesel and leave it on five minutes."

I stare at the bubbling water. "Is it safe?"

"It may tingle. We need to keep it out of his eyes. You get him, I'll get some old towels."

Following the smell back to my room, I find Diesel, head on paws, deep beneath my bed. *I am not coming!*

"You have to!" As I reach for him, he backs away. I get the broom from the kitchen and gently nudge him out, but he gallops off. "Mom, grab him!"

"Where's his collar?"

"We threw it out. Too stinky."

She manages to grab his scruff when his feet slide out from under him. "Diesel, come!" she says, and she drags him over to the tub.

Together we lift him in.

He tries to climb back out.

"Stop, stop!" I push him back.

"Gonna have to buy you a new collar on top of everything," Mom grumbles.

"Morgan might have one. Left over from her dog, King."

"Hmph. You know, every time this dog gets wet, he's going to smell bad again." Mom dumps some of her anti-skunk brew on his fur. "Can you hold him steady?"

"Morgan asked me to a sleepover Tuesday night."

"Morgan this and Morgan that. I thought you couldn't stand her." Mom scrubs at Diesel as he shuffles around in the tub.

Ow, ow, ow! He ducks his head every which way to escape the suds.

I shampoo and massage him, too. No way I can stop him from moving.

Suddenly, his shoulders begin to shift. *I must get the stinging bubbles off!*

I know what's coming. "Cover your eyes!" I yell.

Diesel shakes. Hard. Suds fly everywhere. Onto my face, my arms, my shirt.

While we duck, he makes a break for it.

"Let him run awhile. I've set the timer for five minutes," Mom tells me as she mops up Diesel's mess.

I nuke a wiener and slice it to lure Diesel out from under the bed a second time. It's no use.

That hurt. I don't like pail water. Saucy baths taste better.

"I'm sorry, boy." I reach my arm under the bed as far as it can go and let him have the treat.

He whimpers and licks my fingers, scoops up the wiener, and chews. *Okay.*

I lie there for a while, handing him more slices of wiener.

"Time's up, Naomi. Do you need help getting him out of there?"

"No. I don't think so." I stand up. "Diesel, come. You need to get that stuff off your fur."

The *thunk* of his head hitting the underside of the mattress signals that he's coming out. He slinks behind me.

"We'll just rinse you and then you're done." This time he's not fighting as much, so he feels lighter when we hoist him back into the tub.

He looks at me. *I'm scared.*

"It won't be so bad, I promise. Look I'll come in with you." Mom shakes her head and backs out of the bathroom.

Then, clothes still on, I hop in with Diesel, pull the curtain, and turn the shower on. Second time I've gone in water with all my clothes on. My knees shake as I remember that dive from the dock.

But I wasn't with you. Diesel's thought pops into my head. *You didn't trust.*

Who was there to trust? All those kids who look over my head?

Pizza Girl, he answers.

I sigh. She did try to find me.

We stand under the shower for at least ten minutes. Diesel lets me rub his fur under the water. The water draining off him is brown but the skunk smell seems to be fading.

When I finally shut off the water and pull the curtain back, Mom is standing there, ready with another bucket of hissing bleach brew.

"We're supposed to do this twice."

"No. Diesel's had enough. He had two tomato baths last night."

"If your father had done it right the first time —"

"Dad's not perfect. I get that. But he's a good guy and you know that." I want to say more but stop myself. "You could cut him some slack, you know?"

Mom's mouth sits straight. She doesn't answer.

"And Diesel's just fine the way he is right now."

Morgan's Scheme

The last Monday through, without Diesel, all I wanted to do was stay in bed. I didn't even get up until Mom shook me awake so she could rush me over to Aunt Cathie's to babysit Luanne. But today, bright and early, Morgan shows up at our door.

Morgan has to knee Diesel off her. "Down, boy!"

Wiener Girl, Wiener Girl!

Pizza Girl, no? I think inside my head.

She smells like wieners now. And I have missed her delicious smell!

"C'mon, you just saw Morgan on Saturday," I say out loud.

Forever ago! His tail wags his whole body.

Morgan slides her backpack off and raises a pointer finger. "Sit."

Diesel's butt instantly crashes to the floor. *Pat me. Pat me.*

She crouches down and scrubs behind his ear. "Oh, you're a good, good doggie!"

His tail swishes along the floor. *She likes me.… Oh yes, that's a good spot.* His back leg thumps as she scratches his back. *Love you, love you.* He licks his lips and shifts on his paws.

Traitor. I shake my head at him.

He gives me a sidewise glance. His lips are peeled back like he's smiling. He stands up, and his tail cranks around now, pumping more excitement into him.

"You're such a handsome boy!" Morgan says.

Love you so much! His joy explodes and he jumps on her again, slathering her face.

"Beeehave!" I push at Diesel's head gently to return him to a sit. Then I throw one arm round his neck.

He turns around and laps at my face. *Love you even more! Love, love, love.*

I close my mouth and eyes tightly, leaning away from that tongue.

"Did you dye his fur?"

I open my eyes again.

"It's kind of rosy." Morgan fingers the patch on Diesel's chest, still slightly pink.

"We tomatoed and bleached him to get rid of the skunk smell."

Morgan wrinkles her nose. "Didn't work." She smiles at Diesel. "Highlights his eyes nicely, though."

"Right. Did you bring the collar?"

She takes a worn-out leather band from her backpack and holds it for a moment, frowning. "All I have left of King."

"Sorry." I remember how bad I felt when Diesel died. Four more days to keep him safe or he might die again. "You can have it back as soon as I can buy a new one."

She shakes her head. "I want him to have it. I love Diesel, too." She snaps the collar around his neck.

"Thanks." I give her a half hug and then break away awkwardly. "Come on into the kitchen."

Morgan turns off her moment of sadness like a light switch. "Listen, we have to go shopping."

Walkies, walkies?

"No! I have to learn how to swim." I release Diesel as we head for the kitchen. "Besides I'm having breakfast right now."

Swimming, swimming?

"Later!" I answer him out loud.

"Great. 'Cause you're gonna love this." Morgan suddenly looks around. "Where's your mother?"

"She took some things to my aunt's on her way to work. Listen, you know about giving parents romantic time?"

"Remember, I told you that didn't work. Especially if your dad doesn't come up with the idea himself."

"Right." I fold my arms across my chest. "I want to try anyway. Tuesday night when I come to your house."

"Fine. But he'll only be romantic 'cause you arranged it. Then he'll go back to being boring with her. For our plans it works, though. Like it was meant to be!"

Meant to be. Something in me freezes when she puts it like that. *What else is meant to be?* I glance at my watch. Still flashing.

"You *need* a new swimming suit."

"Yeah, I know." I sit down at the table, and she pulls out a chair across from me. "But my parents are broke."

Walkies, swimming?

"Look at these muffins! I never get anything this good at home." Morgan takes a cranberry lemon one and bites in, chewing for an extra-long time.

Muffins, muffins?

"A bit dry, aren't they? Can I have some milk?"

"They're day-olds from Mom's work." I stand up and pour her a glass from the fridge.

"Don't get me wrong." She shrugs her shoulders as I hand it to her. "They're still tasty." She takes a couple more bites and washes them down with the milk. "We have to take the brat with us to the mall, don't we?"

"Well, Diesel can't watch her. But never mind, I don't have any money." I eat the last bit of my own apple walnut muffin. "How am I supposed to buy a new bathing suit?"

Morgan chews. "Your college fund," she says around her muffin.

I squint at her.

"Don't look at me like that. This is an investment in your future. Your happiness. Wait till I tell you."

"I'm all ears."

"Just so happens I invited the cool girls to a little pool get-together tomorrow night." Morgan gives me her full-toothed grin.

"You did what?" Diesel barks a warning, and I lower my voice. "Who?"

"Tara, Francesca, Brenna, and Su-Ling." She squeals then, very un-Morgan like. "They said yes!"

The ones who, in my other world, didn't notice me drowning at the dock. I frown, sand-in-my-teeth irritated. "Are you even allowed?"

"Why not? It's only a few people. Using the pool helps the water circulate, and think of it, if we get in with the cool girls, our high school year is made."

Then I do stop and imagine these girls as friends. Will I even be alive for September? Especially if I never learn to swim?

But if they really see and take notice of me, I should be safe even if I fall in the water at some dock. Which I will never go near if I can help it. Those girls won't let a friend drown, will they? Soda-pop bubbles of excitement fizz inside me. To have them on my side when others hurl balls at me in gym class or call me pipsqueak and peanut. The cool girls. I can be one of them. I will really be alive then. I sigh.

Morgan takes the last muffin. "Can your mom score us some donuts for the party?"

"You said a few people. Don't think she'll let me go to a party. Not if there's no parents."

"See how perfect? You wanting a sleepover tomorrow? She won't know."

"But I need to learn how to swim. I don't have a lot of time left, Morgan. We can't go shopping today."

"Your whole life you didn't learn, and suddenly now you're in a rush?" She sighs. "We'll go over early tomorrow. Who knows? Maybe with a new bathing suit, you'll have a breakthrough."

A new bathing suit. My mouth puckers. Even before Dad moved out, I found it hard to spend money. Saving seemed like something that could keep us from falling apart. Mom and Dad would still be together if he hadn't spent so much. But medical school seems far away now, and my bathing suit is dorky and worn out. I can't let anyone else see me in it.

"Okay." I surprise even myself. "I'll take the money from my account." Money isn't everything, after all. If Diesel and I stay alive over these next four days, that's what really counts.

"Um, how much do I need?" I ask.

"A dozen. Oh, you mean for the bathing suit. Twenty, um, thirty … forty bucks max." Morgan grins. "They're having a sidewalk sale at the mall. Just bring your debit card."

"No. I only use cash like Money Lady on TV says. That way I stick to a budget."

"Money Lady?" She rolls her eyes. "Whatever!"

Morgan waits as I head upstairs to dig out the card from my underwear drawer. I wave it as I return to the kitchen, then slide it into my wallet. Which is when I notice my watch again. I frown.

"What, you have someplace more important to go?" Morgan asks.

Swimming, I think but shake my head. "My watch keeps flashing the same date and time. Thursday, July first, four thirty."

"Who cares? Honestly, who wears a watch these days?"

"My father gave it to me."

"So get a new battery!"

"You know that dream I told you about where I drown?"

"Your second-sight dream?"

"Uh huh." I tap my watch. "This was the time I drowned at."

Her mouth drops open and she stares at me. For just one moment, I think she believes me and understands. She'll change her mind and we'll have a swimming lesson like she promised. Then she shakes her head.

"Stop eating sweets before bed, I'm tellin' ya." She winks. "And that way there'll be more donuts for the rest of us."

14

Monday, June 28:

Bikini Shopping

After I finish breakfast, I lead Diesel down to the cool of the basement and turn on the television to the Super Dog finals. I put out a large bowl of water. He won't even have to climb the stairs if he gets thirsty. Not like last time I left him, in the yard with nothing. "We're heading for the mall. Dogs are not allowed."

"Aroooh!" He slumps down in disgust.

I kneel down and pat him. "I'm sorry, Diesel."

Alone. His toffee eyes fill with sadness.

"I'll give you a treat."

Okay! He thumps his tail.

I slip him a sliver of wiener left over from yesterday, still in my pocket. He swallows it and drops his mouth open in a relaxed pant.

I give him one last pat goodbye.

Then Morgan and I head off to pick up Baby Luanne. By the time we have her diapered and dressed and all the buckles done up in the stroller, it's getting close to her nap time. Her head nods as we set off for the bus stop. Dead asleep by the time the bus comes, but it turns out strollers aren't allowed unless they're folded up.

"You do not want this kid awake, trust me." Morgan manages to convince the driver the stroller won't block the aisles, and for once I'm glad for her mouth.

A block before the mall we climb down the back stairs of the bus, Morgan carrying the wheel rod of the stroller and me holding the handle. The doors fold closed behind us as we head for my bank, Luanne still sleeping.

Withdrawing from an ATM makes me feel tense. I'm spending money, after all, drawing from my safety nest egg. It's been so long, I have to think about my birthdate password. Is it month, day, year or day, month, year? My fingers tremble as I finally count three crisp twenties fresh from the machine.

"What's wrong now?" Morgan asks when I stare at them.

"I need this money to go to medical school. My parents can't even afford rent." I look down at my watch. Will I even get to go to school?

"You're a brain." She pats my head. "You'll get a scholarship."

She's so irritating. I duck from her hand. Can I win a scholarship? I can't even learn how to swim. But she's still right about the bathing suit. I can't be seen in public in Little Mermaid anymore.

We power march the rest of the way to the mall, me anxious that I'll back out if we don't hurry. If we slow down, Luanne might wake up, too.

The parking lot looks full, and the moment we step through the doors the air conditioning blasts us. Racks of clothing and tables with markdowns line the halls. Too many people crowd and paw through the offerings.

"Let's go to Economart. That's where Aunt Cathie gets all her bargains." I don't wait for an answer, just steer the stroller in that direction.

"Where do you think you're going?" Morgan asks as we pass through the open door of the store and I head toward the children's department. "The ladies' department is in that corner."

"Ladies' won't have my size," I tell her. She follows me to a rack of strawberry and banana-coloured suits, some of them with Disney Princesses on them, others with Paw Patrol. "What about this one?" I hold up a deeply discounted yellow suit with a blue Cookie Monster grinning from the middle.

"You are not wearing kiddie characters. Even if we have to go to a special midget shop."

"Midget, Morgan? Really. You mean a boutique for petites."

"Whatever." Morgan grabs the stroller away from me and forces me to follow her over to browse the ladies' corner.

A *40%-OFF* sign draws my attention. I shuffle through racks of boulder-holder bra-style tops and circus-tent skirts and bottoms. This shouldn't be so hard!

"Over here!" Morgan hisses from a rack of tankinis.

Better choice there. Leopard prints, black spandex with zippers all over, blue denim shorts and halter tops. Frantically, I check the tags — all size ten and up. "Too big, too big," I tell Morgan as I slide them across the rack.

"What size do you wear?"

"I don't know. Zero?"

"Ohmigosh. How can you be a size nothing? Everybody has to be a size something." She steps back from the bathing suits and tosses up her hands.

But I've been such a small nothing for so long. Peanut, as Morgan and Simon call me.

"Maybe I'm bigger. I've grown a little."

"Let's try Bikini Island."

I frown. "Isn't that store super pricey?"

"Not when there's a sidewalk sale."

"Okay." We make our way over to the glass elevator in the centre of the mall and, as we step on, the cool girls suddenly appear, giggling as they squeeze in. Batting their eyelashes and waving their glossy, pointed nails, they grip bags of their fashion finds. Tara, Francesca, Brenna, and Su-Ling surround us in a forest of long legs and hair. Unbelievably beautiful. Their giggles and cherry-lip, lemony-hair smell fill the air.

Su-Ling nods and gives me a small smile.

She noticed me! I smile back.

"Can't wait for the party tomorrow night," Francesca says to Morgan. "Who else is coming?"

"Oh, it will be a surprise," Morgan answers, loud and braggy.

I squint at her and she winks back.

Francesca laughs. The others join in. I can't believe it. Everybody wants to be them or at least close to them. Morgan's done it. Got us set for high school.

That's if Diesel and I find a way to survive the summer.

Luanne stirs.

"Shhh, shh. There, there," I say.

The ride ends and as soon as the doors swish open, the girls push past us with little hand waves.

Quiet again, but too late. Luanne squawks awake.

Oh, great. She's crying. Waking up early has put her in a mood.

We move quickly toward the store at the end of the passage where two inflated green palm trees stand on either side of the door. Bikini Island calls us.

Monday, June 28:

With Strings Attached

By the time we reach those palm trees, Luanne's shrieking parts the crowds around us. "What do we do?" Morgan asks.

"Give her something." I fumble in my bag and hand her my keys.

She jangles them a few times and then flings them into the store. I run to pick them up.

"Aww!" A girl with spiky black hair and a rhinestone nose stud steps from behind the counter to talk to Luanne. "Whatsa matter, baby?"

Luanne loves sparkly, and she stops mid-sob to stare at that nose.

"Can she have a candy?" The girl is already unwrapping a bright green sucker. She holds it out. Too bad if I say no.

Luanne bobs up and down in her stroller, reaching for the candy. Will she choke on it? If I take it away now, she may work herself up too much. Which can't be good for her heart.

Or our shopping. Luanne quiets down, so that settles it.

"Can you help us?" Morgan asks the salesgirl. "We're looking for something extra, extra, extra small."

I shrug my shoulders. "I don't really know my size."

The girl taps her nose above the rhinestone. "Let's measure you."

She whips out a tape measure from her pocket and wraps it around my hips. She clicks her tongue and shakes her head.

"That bad, huh?" Morgan says.

"You probably still have some growing to do." Next she wraps the tape measure around my chest. I breathe in deeply to expand as much as possible, but she frowns. "Let's be generous. You're a size four."

I grin, relieved. A big promotion from size zero!

"With strings, you can tie everything tighter anyway." Her mouth twists around as she chews on that information. "We did have some." Nose tapping again. "So much of our stock is gone now with the end of summer. Let me just see."

The end of summer? It's not even July, I think as we follow her to the rack at the back of the store. This store only sells beachwear. Are there back-to-school bathing suits coming soon?

She begins sliding the bikinis back, one by one, as she checks the tags. "No, no, no. Mmm, mmm, mmm." Her lips fold over in a straight line. She pauses at a red two-piece with no tag and flips the fabric to find the label. "Here's one!" She hands it to me, triumphant. "On sale, too! Forty percent off."

I stare at the sunset-red scraps of cloth.

"Try it on." Morgan gives me a shove toward the changing room.

What choice do I have? I step into a nearby stall and switch from my shorts into the swimsuit bottom, which ends just below my belly button.

Then I slip on the two triangles and tie the string around my neck. Oh great, how do I tie the back?

"How you making out?" the salesgirl calls.

"Morgan! Help me!" I open the lock with one hand while holding my top closed at the back with the other. She's going to make fun of me; I can't even dress myself. I step outside.

"Here, allow me." The salesgirl reaches around my back and ties the strings up tightly. "You're in luck. These tops look fab on flat girls."

"Guess you would know," Morgan says.

I want to hug her.

"You'd never catch them making clothes men can't close themselves," Morgan grumbles.

The salesgirl ignores her. "Dynamite colour for you! Fits nice, too."

I look in the mirror. Gasp.

"Take it!" Morgan commands. "It looks great!"

I quickly change back into my clothes and carry the bikini to the counter.

"How much is it?" I ask.

"No tag, let me just check. They were a hundred twenty dollars …"

One hundred and twenty dollars!

"Less forty percent … that makes …"

"Seventy-two dollars before tax," I tell her as she scans the calculations on her chart. For a couple of stretchy red scraps. "I'm sorry. I only have sixty." Quickly, I take the stroller and push Luanne through the exit.

"You have to have that bikini," Morgan hisses after me.

"You said it would cost forty dollars max!" I hiss back.

"Who cares? I'm going back to get it for you."

Luanne begins waving the white stick of her sucker around, squawking again.

"You're not stealing it," I call, loud so she can hear me over Luanne's noise. Heads turn toward us.

"Can-dy!" Luanne wails, showing her empty sucker stick to anyone who looks at her.

"What?" Morgan shrieks.

"You heard me."

Even her rust-fleck freckles pale. "I … don't … steal."

Luanne wails and more heads turn, even as we keep moving.

"Come on." I lower my voice. "At the convenience store you —"

"Pay for everything I take. Like I told you before. Just 'cause the guy there thinks all teenagers steal doesn't mean you should believe him."

"Shh, shh," I tell Luanne. "Do you want a nice juice?" I fumble for a box in my bag.

Morgan holds two twenties in my face. "Uncle Lurch gave me money for helping him clean one of his other pools."

"And you want to lend it to me?" Luanne reduces her sobs to loud inhales as I pop the straw into the juice box.

"If you're going to high school, you're going to have to stop dressing like a toddler."

"You're so insulting." I bend to hand Luanne her drink and then straighten again. "C'mon."

"What's it going to be?" Morgan pushes the money toward me again. "Little Mermaid or knock-'em-dead red?"

Knock 'em dead? I push the money back. "No, thank you."

"Uh! You are so frustrating!" Morgan tucks the money away again.

"No. I'm not." I glance back at the shop. "You take Luanne over to the food court. I'm going back for it." I take a deep breath. "Going to use my debit card."

"Woohoo! You won't be sorry! Those girls are gonna be our besties." Morgan smiles.

I look down at my watch and shiver. Still *THU*, still *July 01*, still *4:30*. The exact time I dove into water around those girls and it didn't end well. But they'll watch out for me, now that they know I exist. Everything should be fine. Maybe Morgan's right about my time counter. "Afterward, Morgan, let's pop into Batteries-R-Us and get my watch fixed."

Monday, June 28:

Life Counter

The watch battery checks out fine in the store — the numbers just will not budge. Our life counter, Diesel calls it. It'll work once he saves me. But I'm not going to jump off any dock again, so he'll never need to, and I should be able to just throw the watch away. Somehow I can't. It would feel like tossing away my life preserver.

Also, it would feel like I'm giving up on Dad and his dorky presents. How can I hope Mom will take him back if I give up, too? A lucky charm for Dad, and in a few days it will tell the right time, even for just one moment. So I keep wearing it.

It's a great day anyway, with finding my first adult bathing suit that fits. I start to believe maybe I *can* learn to swim.

To top it off, just like the last Monday through, Mom brings home a supermarket rotisserie chicken that comes with bread, fries, and coleslaw. "A picnic in a bag," she says, on special for less than she can make it herself.

Diesel wags his tail enthusiastically. *It smells so good.* He can't help himself — *Let me get a closer whiff* — and he jumps up on her.

"Down, boy." She bumps him gently with her knee.

He drops but tilts his head from one side to the other. *Chicken?*

"Go!" Mom points away from herself.

"Not for you, boy," I tell him.

Diesel drops his head and paces behind her, toenails clicking on the floor, as she finishes unbagging the food and setting it on the table.

Napkins, ketchup, salt, vinegar. She hums, in a good mood for a change. Maybe it's the holiday from cooking in the heat.

But then the doorbell rings. "Rawf!" Diesel's tail cranks hard as he scuttles toward the door. *Someone is at the front.*

Dad walks in, an empty brown box tucked under each arm. That did not happen last time. "I'm here to pack the books," he calls from the hall. "I know they're the heaviest to carry."

Mom lifts an eyebrow. "What a surprise."

I can hear between the lines: *You should have called first.*

"Please, Mom, please," I beg her in a low voice, "give him a break."

She steps out of the kitchen into the hallway.

"Woof!" *Welcome, Alpha!*

Dad puts the boxes down for a moment to take Diesel's head in his hands and scratch around his cheeks and ears. He looks up at Mom. "Do you want me to take the boxes over to Cathie's right away?"

"No," Mom says in one down note. "She says she has no room for them. You can take them directly to the recycle centre."

"What? Not our books! I'll take them to my brother's. Save them for when we get a new place."

Mom doesn't contradict him. Instead she smiles. Morgan's so wrong. Dad and Mom love their books. They were meant to be with each other. I give Dad the eyeball and nod to remind him.

"Also, tomorrow night?" he says. "I have *The Shape of Water* reserved from the library. Won best picture. Remember you wanted to see it?" He smiles. "Leo's TV doesn't work very well or I'd invite you over. Unless ... we could both watch it here." He turns and winks at me.

"I don't know. I have so much packing and so little time."

"We'll do it together. After the movie."

"Fine."

"Great. Don't let me disturb you," Dad says and heads for the living room bookshelf.

I will accompany Alpha. Diesel abandons the good food smell to stay on Dad's heels.

I set the table with a couple of plates and forks and knives, for Mom and me only, not daring to push my luck.

Chicken! Diesel returns, tongue hanging out as he eyes the table.

Dad checks in with us a few seconds later, loaded down with a box filled with books. "Taking these to the car. I'll be back for the other box in a second."

"You could have supper with us, James," Mom says, barely turning her head.

He sets the box down and wipes his brow. "I don't want to impose."

"We're going to have plenty of leftovers as it is. Just grab a plate and some cutlery."

Dad hesitates for a breath. Then he smiles. "Thank you." Dad has excellent white teeth that light up the room when they're on exhibit like that. "Let me get this box out first. And wash up."

He whistles as he leaves the house. "My Girl," I think the tune is called.

My mother sings along under her breath.

He bounds outside and in again and then I hear the taps. Back in the kitchen, he fills the door frame. A handsome guy, my dad. Wish I'd inherited his height. He sits down opposite me with his cutlery and a plate, which Mom fills with chicken and coleslaw. I already have mine.

Diesel shifts on his feet and whimpers. *Will there be no food for me?*

You'll get your kibble after.

Kibble! He slumps down in disgust.

"Eat before it gets cold," Mom tells me.

I bite into the crispy, salty skin; the dark meat melts under my tongue. Last time through, I could barely eat anything and it all tasted like nothing.

Diesel focuses his large toffee eyes on my mouth. I take another bite. He whimpers again, stands up, and nudges my knee. *Please!* I look around, then quietly slip him some of the skin.

"Don't feed the dog from the table," Mom orders. "You'll only encourage him to beg."

I won't beg if you just give it to me.

I shrug at Diesel, who slumps down a second time, head between his paws. "Arowww!"

I'll save you some, I tell him in my head. Then I eat my coleslaw, super sweet and mushy, just the way I like it. The bread is pale white, and as I smooth the square of butter across it, the fresh dough squishes down.

"Mmm, mmm. I am enjoying this meal with my family," Dad says. "'Course, your salad is way better, Adele."

"Uh huh." Mom's left eyebrow stretches. "I thought you didn't like the way I put broccoli in my coleslaw."

"Really? Did I say that?" Dad leans toward Mom and gives her his puppy eyes. "'Cause I miss broccoli in my life." He reaches for her hand.

She smiles but bats his hand away. "Oh now, stop! You do not."

Oh yes, he does! I think about our wiener roast on paper plates.

Dad opens his mouth, but the phone rings.

Diesel barks. *Thing on the wall calling!*

It rings again, and we all look in that direction. But Mom has a rule: we don't answer during meals.

"Probably just somebody wanting to sell us something," Mom says.

It rings again. "Wouff! Wouff!"

"Telemarketer," Dad agrees. "The only job most people can get." He stabs at his chicken with his fork and waves it at the phone. "Poor guy on the other end probably gets paid by the call."

"Not like we can afford anything he's selling." Mom purses her lips and frowns as the phone gives its final ring.

"We don't need duct cleaning anyway," Dad answers.

"No need to bother people at dinner," Mom says. "Lots of jobs at the Donut Time. Shoulda seen the lineup of cars this afternoon. All those engines running."

"People should just walk in. Have some real face time." It looks like Dad is agreeing again. "Don't need the internet for that."

'Course, Dad recently argued with Mom that we should get internet in the house so I could do my homework better and he could job search from home.

Things are going so well. Still, I'm afraid Mom will launch into how his job hunting is going. So I try to change the topic. "This chicken is nice and moist." I scoop the last bit from my plate into my mouth and then serve myself some more.

"Well, look at your appetite. Maybe you're growing," Dad says, reaching across the table to ruffle my hair.

I shrug my shoulders. "I wish."

"Why don't we have ice cream for dessert?" Mom says, patting my shoulder. She heads for the freezer and takes a container out.

Cold creamy food? Diesel paws at one of my knees.

Sorry! I look down at him. *Dairy's not good for dogs.*

"Aroough!"

"We have this new flavour the shop is promoting. Coconut toffee crunch." She scoops some out into two parfait dishes and I pass Dad one, along with a spoon. I take the other.

"You not having any, Adele?"

"I am trying to watch my figure," Mom says.

"Why don't you just let me do that?" Dad says. "From where I'm sitting, you're looking pretty good."

Mom blushes but doesn't say anything.

"This flavour is yummy," I tell her. I savour mine, allowing it to melt in my mouth and cool me down. I hit a toffee chunk and chew it a little before swallowing.

Dad nods. "Delicious. Here, try some of mine." He leans toward Mom and offers her a spoonful.

She takes it.

"Good, right? You really not going to have some?"

She shakes her head.

He shakes his head, too, then crosses his arms and leans back in the chair. "Naomi, your mom told me you've bought yourself a new bathing suit."

"I couldn't help noticing the Bikini Island bag you carried into your room," Mom explains.

"*Bikini* Island? Why don't you model it for us?" Dad says, his voice a bit gravelly.

Oh, oh. That gravel tells me Dad doesn't like the idea of a two-piece. "Let me just finish." Delaying, I continue to eat slowly. Then I scrape at the last milky spots and lick the spoon. Absolutely nothing left. Both Mom and Dad sit, waiting and watching.

Finally, I head into my room, Diesel padding at my heels. He sprawls out across the floor as I empty my Bikini Island bag. The bill tumbles out, *NO RETURN* stamped across it in red. Not a big surprise. It's kind of like underwear so close to your body. Who would want to wear a used swimsuit? I'm not taking it back anyway, I tell myself firmly. Bought it with my own money, after all. I take off all my clothes, step into the bright-red bottom and pull it up. This time I tie the top at the back first and then arrange the tiny triangles across my chest. It takes some fumbling to knot the string at the top of my neck — it needs to be tied pretty tight.

After a few moments, I stand back and look in the mirror. The long smooth expanse of skin between the top and bottom makes me look taller, slinkier. Great!

So why do my feet not move me back to the kitchen? They stay glued to the hardwood floor. Is there too much skin showing?

"Are you coming, Naomi?" Mom calls. "Your dad has to leave."

I find my flip-flops and slip them on. Then, *slap, slap, slap*, back I head. Behind me, *click, click, click*, Diesel follows.

"Oh my." Mom covers her mouth with her hand.

Dad, with his second box of books in his arms, stumbles back and gasps. "A bikini!" He drops the box. "Red?"

"Two-pieces are the only kind that fit me, Dad."

"It's beautiful." Mom's on my side!

"I don't care! It doesn't cover you enough. You'll get skin cancer."

Diesel barks along with Dad's yelling. *Angry Alpha Male! Danger!* "Rawf! Rawf!"

Mom speaks softly. "I was wearing a red bathing suit just like that when we first met. Remember?" She smiles, just with her lips. Still, she looks happy for a moment, like she's enjoying that memory.

"That's exactly it! I don't want guys looking at her. I want better for Naomi." He flings his arms wide open. "She should go to university till she has every degree and diploma there is. She should become a doctor … of everything." His hands drop, his shoulders with them. "She shouldn't end up with a loser like me."

"Rawf!"

The ranting and barking stop, and there is a moment of silence when the world stops turning. Mom looks at Dad. First her mouth puckers, then her lips part. She is going to say something.

I think of all the great things she could say: *You're anything but a loser, James. That was the happiest day of my life.* How about *Things didn't work out so bad. Look at the lovely daughter we have.* If she says any of these things, the packed suitcase she flung onto the porch might be emptied back into the closet upstairs again. Our family can be put back together.

But before any words can leave her lips, Dad picks up the second box of books and walks out the door.

Alpha in exile again! "Rawf! Rawf!"

The world pauses midspin for another moment.

"Mom, it was the only bathing suit in my size. Honest."

"You're young. You can wear a bikini," she answers. "Your dad just has to get over himself."

Still, I feel bad. Does this mean their Tuesday movie night is off 'cause they disagree? All I want — besides me, Diesel, and Baby Luanne staying alive — is for Mom and Dad to get back together.

"You know I was planning to go into nursing when I met your father," Mom says.

"Why didn't you anyway? Dad didn't make you stop."

"No." Mom smiles. "We had you, instead. Best thing that ever happened to me. But I was planning to go back to school, now that you're so grown-up. Then your father lost his job."

"Oh, Mom! We can still find a way."

"Sure we can." She smiles again. "So you just enjoy that beautiful bathing suit. Don't worry about your father."

Later in bed I think all of this over again. Morgan talked me into buying the knock-'em-dead red that caused all this trouble. Should I keep wearing my butt-worn Little Mermaid? Stuff the two-piece in my drawer? But I can't dress like a kid if I'm going into high school. I need to wear that bikini. How can Dad object when there are no men at the private pool where Morgan and I swim? And I'll wear sunscreen.

Hopefully Dad and Mom will still watch *The Shape of Water* together. I heard it's a super-romantic love story.

Eyes closed, I picture myself lounging at the edge of the pool, then standing, tall and slim in the knock-'em-dead red, offering some donut bits to the cool girls, breathing in the evening air. I inhale deeply, imagining it, but smell disgusting dog fart instead. "Oh, Diesel!" The odour takes me out of my dream. Can there be anything worse? Maybe dog fart combined with a hint of bitter tomato and skunk.

I roll over, covering my head with a pillow to try to block out the smell.

Tuesday, June 29:

Knock-'Em-Dead Red

Next morning, standing in front of the mirror, I smooth my hands over my body and bikini, and they feel like one. Did Mom look like me when she was my age? I know Mom and Dad fell in love when they were really young.

Diesel crawls out from under the bed, paw over paw, and wags his approval. *Are we swimming today?*

"Later," I tell him. I frown at myself in the mirror. "I'm a traitor, just when Dad could use my support."

Diesel wags harder. *Breakfast, then?*

"In a minute." I shrug. "Just look at this bathing suit. It's the nicest piece of clothing I own."

Diesel barks sharply. *Breakfast, then to the pool!*

"Not big on fashion, are you?" I shake my head at him. His tail thumps.

The smell of coffee drifts into my room, which tells me Mom's still here. I quickly cover up with cut-off shorts and a T-shirt and rush out to join her, Diesel at my heels. It isn't often that Mom and I can sit down for breakfast together.

"Good morning, Naomi. I brought home yogurt from the shop. Want some?" she asks.

"Sure." Donut Time yogurt has always been my favourite, even before Mom worked there.

No toast again. Diesel slumps down under the table.

"I'll just get the dog some kibble," I say.

Kibble? "Mrouwww!" Diesel yowls his complaint.

I sigh. "And make myself some *toast*, too." Diesel stands up and wags at that word. I slide some bread in the toaster and fill Diesel's bowls with food and water.

"I like the way you're taking responsibility for that animal." Mom plunks a plastic cup in front of me.

"I am getting older, even if I stay pint size." I check the yogurt container. Best-before date is only today. Score! I pull off the lid and remove the divider between the crumbly granola and the yogurt. I dip my spoon through the top layer and taste. Smooth creaminess with a hint of crunch. "By the way, tonight's the night I'm going to Morgan's for a sleepover. Remember?"

"You're still planning that, are you? Even though you don't like her." Mom sips at her coffee while I enjoy a cluster of yogurty blueberries.

"You know, I didn't. But she's teaching me to swim and gave me that collar for Diesel. Helping me train him, too, and well ... maybe she's really not as bad as I thought." As I tell her this, I realize I can't remember the last time Morgan called Luanne "the brat," either. She offered me money to help out with my bathing suit. Even when I was drowning, she was the one person who tried to find me in the water.

"Your father may be coming over with that movie. You sure you don't want to stay and watch it?"

He's still coming! Yay! "No, no. But Mom, is there any way you can bring me home some treats? Donut holes or something? Morgan's got a brother and sister."

"A hostess present. My, that's considerate of you." Mom reaches across the table to pat my shoulder.

Not that considerate. I wince with guilt. It's to feed the cool girls, after all. A little get-together Mom knows nothing about.

"I'll see what's left over after my shift today. You just get me her parents' phone number so that I can talk to them first." She stands up and begins washing our breakfast dishes.

I freeze. "You mean her mom's number?" Does Morgan's mother even know I'm coming? I'll have to check with Morgan first. "They're separated, just like you and Dad."

Mom frowns at me. "Whichever parent's house you're sleeping over at. That phone number." She washes out her coffee cup. "Would you put these away?" She gestures to the drying rack. "I want to get some things together to bring to Cathie's so the move's not so hard."

After I finish stowing the cutlery, Mom and I each grab a box of winter clothes and we stroll toward Aunt Cathie's together, me with Diesel's leash wrapped around my wrist.

"You sure you don't want to leave the dog at home?" Mom asks.

"Oh, you don't need Diesel around when Dad ... I mean, when you're trying to pack."

Mom squints. "True enough, but can *you* manage like that right now?"

"Oh yeah. We've been working on getting Diesel to walk nice. Watch this." We reach the corner and Diesel sits without being told. I slip him a wiener sliver. "Good dog!"

Thank you.

When the coast is clear, we cross to the other side. No yanking.

"My, that is impressive," Mom says.

We walk a little farther, the box getting heavier as we go but Diesel still trotting along nicely.

"Rouff! Rouff!" Suddenly he does yank the leash, so hard I stumble forward and drop the box.

Long-eared thing!

A rabbit springs across the street.

"Ow! My arm, Diesel!" I tug him back. *What is wrong with you? I thought you knew better.*

Long-ears are still a trigger for me. Working on that.

"Lucky your box isn't full of dishes," Mom says as she turns in to Aunt Cathie's driveway.

I pick up the box and catch up with her. "Okay, maybe he's not perfect. But he is much better."

We go in through my aunt's front door and yell hello. "Just putting some boxes in the basement," Mom calls.

When we come back up, I sit down with Luanne while Aunt Cathie and my mom leave for work together. They enjoy each other's company, more like best friends than sisters. Mom couldn't have any more kids after I was born, so no sisters or brothers for me. Luanne fills that gap for both me and Mom. And when she goes in for her heart surgery later this year, we will both be there day and night for her.

The move will be a good thing for all of us, even if Mom has to leave her favourite kitchen. She will come to see that. How Dad will fit in to this will be the big question. Will he fit in again?

Luanne offers me a Cheerio from her high chair. Diesel wags hopefully from a perfect sit at my feet.

I take it. "Mmm."

Throw one to me. "Rawf!"

Suddenly, Luanne bobs up and down wildly at something behind me. "Gun, gun, gun!"

Wiener Girl has arrived. Diesel wags at high speed.

I turn and see Morgan's face at the side door. *Luanne calls her Gun now?*

"Sit!" I hold out a finger to warn Diesel as I walk over and unlock the door. "You're early."

Diesel's haunches touch the floor for barely an instant, and then he throws himself at Morgan.

"Nothing better to do," she says as she pushes him away. "Down," she tells Diesel and his haunches drop. "Guess you didn't bring any of those muffins over."

"No, but Mom said she'd bring home something for our sleepover."

"Who's a good, good doggie?" Morgan baby-talks at Diesel as she scrubs around his head with her fingers. She lowers her own face so he can lick it. Luanne waves a Cheerio at Morgan and she takes it.

"About the sleepover, Mom insists on calling your house."

"Fine. My mother knows." Morgan takes another Cheerio from Luanne's outstretched hand.

"What is she going to say about the pool party?"

"Nothing. We're going for a swim. We're not staying out late or anything." Morgan spoons some Cheerios into Luanne's mouth. Diesel scarfs up the ones that drop along the way.

Crunchy sweet. Yum.

"Mom wouldn't like it that we're partying with no adults."

"We're swimming with friends, that's all. Which is true, right? You worry too much."

"No. I just anticipate. That way there are no problems later."

"How's that workin' for you?" She feeds Luanne some more cereal.

I think about how much I worry about money and the future. What if I had really drowned at the dock? Would any of it have mattered? "Not great, actually."

"Okay, then. So let's do it my way. Does your aunt have anything else to eat? I don't really like cereal."

I check the fridge. "I see bread. You want some toast?"

Yes. Diesel barks sharply.

Diesel has always known that word. I stare at him for a moment. Has he always understood everything? Is it just me who hasn't listened to him? I take the butter and jam out of the fridge, then slide some bread into the toaster.

When Morgan starts nibbling at the breakfast I've made her, I suggest she give some of the crust to Diesel.

"Shake," she says, offering him a red corner. "Shake." She holds out her hand.

Oh fine. I will do this for you. He lays his paw on top. *Now food?*

She lets him have the crust.

Jammy. Good.

The next one she balances on his nose, holding out her finger and counting. On three, she tells him, "Okay, go," and he snaps it up.

"Wow. I wish I had started training him earlier."

"What difference does it make? You're training him now."

"Maybe I just wish I'd paid more attention." I glance at my watch. Even though the numbers and date never change, I feel like my time might be running out. I shake my head. Depressing thoughts.

"You still wearing that thing? I thought we agreed that eating chocolate gives you bad dreams. Period," Morgan says.

"*You* agreed. I told you, my dad gave it to me. I can't just throw it away." There's a catch in my throat like I want to cry, but I don't want to, really I don't.

She pats my back. Sympathy pat. I'm embarrassed. "Don't worry. In just two days, your watch is gonna have its moment." She chuckles.

Two days, two days. Exactly why I worry. My thoughts jump on a hamster wheel as I think about Thursday. I drowned at the time flashing on my watch. But in that other life Diesel died, too, so that's changed, gone a different way, whatever the watch does or doesn't do. We trained Diesel. He shouldn't chase after cars or squirrels anymore. Besides, I take him wherever I go and I pay closer attention to him, too.

Now, all I have to do is learn how to swim and not jump off any docks. Better yet, not go near any lake at all.

"Let's clean up here and get going," I tell Morgan. "Maybe with the knock-'em-dead red on I'll finally be able to swim."

She grins, big white teeth showing. Then she gathers up the plates. I wash and she dries while Luanne pitches Cheerios for Diesel to catch.

Afterward, we snap the leash on a dog who sits so calmly, he looks as well trained as the agility dogs on television. As we step out the door, carrying Luanne's stroller over the steps together, I feel almost as safe as I did before hitting my head. Plus, I like having a friend to help with this stuff. Maybe I don't have a sister like Mom, but I do have Morgan.

Which makes two friends, counting Diesel. And all this time I thought I liked being alone.

The heat blasts us the moment we step outside, and the sky holds the murky grey of a high pollution count, but still I walk straighter and feel taller as we head toward the wealthier side of town. Diesel trots alongside beautifully and Luanne doesn't squawk. When we arrive at the house, I don't feel like I'm sneaking in anymore. I stride to the gate and push through the moment Morgan unlocks it.

On the other side, I can't wait to strip down to my new suit. Off come the shorts and top in about three beats. Diesel sits at attention, tall and still, the whole while. At the pool, Morgan takes out some inflatable water wings from her bag. "Not for you, don't worry." She slides them onto Luanne's arms and puts her mouth to the valve to blow. "You can keep them. My little brother can swim on his own now."

So I should be able to learn today, too.

Diesel barks his approval.

Once the wings are fully inflated, Morgan steps down into the water, holding Luanne's hand. I follow. When the water reaches my chest, Diesel jumps in to swim with us, dog-paddling in a large circle around me. *Keep safe.*

"Pew!" Morgan waves her hand in front of her nose. "The water's bringing out the skunk again."

"Who cares? We're outside anyway." He'll save me if something should go wrong.

Luanne shrieks with happiness as she practises big arms with Morgan.

Diesel barks. *Hurray! The small one swims.*

"Look how great Luanne is doing," Morgan says. "Kick, kick, kick," she tells Luanne as she moves the baby's legs with her hands.

No tone. No other meaning. Morgan really seems impressed. And she's using Luanne's actual name now.

Luanne moves her feet and arms way better than I can. "Maybe I *should* get water wings." Pushing out the water with my hands while kicking my legs at the same time doesn't seem to be working any better today.

"Why don't you try swimming underwater?" Morgan suggests as she scoops Luanne into her arms.

"Really? I thought the whole point was to stay on top."

Morgan grabs my hand. "Come over here. It's easier." She drags me to the deep end. When I hesitate, she puts her hand on top of my head — "One, two, three, dunk!" — and pushes me down.

At first I struggle. Try to kick her. I want to kill her, really. I'm drowning right this minute. Doesn't matter what my watch says.

But then I decide. Now or never. I put my hands together into an arrow and push out; my legs frog-kick behind. It works! The movement sends me forward. Through the wavering water, the world of legs and paws appears blobby and slow. I keep moving. If I can stay below like this, everything will stay perfect. I can swim.

Swimming, swimming. Diesel stays right beside me. I feel safe.

But of course I have to come up for air. When I finally surface to take a breath, Morgan and Luanne cheer and clap.

I forget about my watch; I can't help smiling. Underwater, I can do it! Maybe I can even save myself at the lake if I ever jump off a pier again. "Woohoo!" I fist-bump with Morgan.

We're making too much noise, though, because the wrinkled apple-doll face pokes out of the upstairs window next door.

"That dog shouldn't be in the pool. He's going to tear the liner," she crabs down at us.

"Yeah, well, the pool is cement. So no worries," Morgan answers back.

"I'm going to call the police." The old lady's head tucks back into the house, like a turtle head sucked back into its shell.

"You do that," Morgan calls to her. "We're leaving anyway."

Using Up Our Good Luck

Morgan takes her time, but I scramble out of the pool quickly, anxious to get out of there.

"So what do you want to do now?" she asks. "Wanna come to my house?"

"Rouww, rouww, rouww!" *I want to come.*

"That's okay, Diesel. You're invited." Morgan scratches behind his ear. "Our family misses King a lot since we had to put him down."

Can she hear Diesel's thoughts, too, now?

My bathing suit is wet, but I just throw my clothes over it 'cause I'm in a hurry. Who knows if that woman has actually called the police? "Let's hang out at my aunt's so Luanne can have her nap in her own crib."

Morgan stands up and Diesel leaps to his paws. I tuck Luanne into her stroller.

Once we're out of the yard, I feel a lot better.

At Aunt Cathie's we sit down for lunch and Baby Luanne nods off in the middle of her crackers and cheese. The bigger miracle is that as I carry her to her crib and for the long drop down to the mattress, she stays asleep. When I check Aunt Cathie's cupboard, I find a supply of popcorn.

Warm, crunchy things! Diesel wags like crazy.

Turns out my aunt also has a copy of *Wonder Woman* and we get to watch the whole movie without a peep out of Luanne.

Even more miraculous, Aunt Cathie comes home early and pays me for two weeks of babysitting. Must have something to do with Mom sharing the rent next month. That for sure didn't happen on the last Tuesday through. Now I can replace the money I withdrew from the bank, with interest!

But are we using up all our luck? Something prickles at the back of my neck. Can we make it last past that four thirty time slot in two days? As we leave my aunt's house together, Morgan grabs Diesel's leash. Standing on the sidewalk, I hesitate. Diesel sits at attention, one ear up.

"So now I just need to go home for some things. Do you want to come in and wait for my mom to see if she brought anything for the party?"

Morgan grins. "Yeah, that would be good. Hope she got us some of those sour-cream-glazed bits."

I would enjoy any kind of sweet treats. Diesel wags again.

We start walking. "I don't know. They're pretty popular. She only brings what's left at the end of the day."

"There's nothing that's not my favourite," Morgan answers. "Anything will be great."

"Did I tell you Dad is bringing *The Shape of Water* to watch with Mom tonight? She's been wanting to see that forever."

"What? That creepy movie where the mute lady falls in love with a lizard man?"

"It won best picture."

"Doesn't matter. No sane woman dreams of living underwater with a reptile. She's not going to want to cuddle up to your father watching that!"

Everything else in my life seems to be clicking into place. Can't this one night go right for Dad, too? I trip over a crack in the sidewalk.

"You okay?" Morgan grabs my arm so that I won't fall all the way down.

Break your mother's back — the kiddie rhyme comes back to me. Maybe it will be Dad who breaks his back.

"Yeah." I continue as if nothing happened. "Do you really think those girls will be our friends when school starts?"

"Yup. What are you worried about? Not like you're wearing little princess clothes today. You're gonna look like a grown-up!"

"My father hates my bikini." We turn up the walkway to my house.

"That's a good sign." Morgan winks, something she hasn't done since yesterday. "Dads never like anything that attracts boys."

We go inside, and soon Mom arrives, loaded with two boxes of treats, plenty for all: cream- and jam-filled donuts, sour-cream glazed, crullers, and muffins. Plus some of the mini-bits.

Mmm. Sweet smells. Diesel lies down close to Mom's feet, like he hopes to trip her and score some goodies for himself.

"How many brothers and sisters do you have?" Mom asks Morgan.

"Two, one of each. It's me who really loves donuts, Mrs. Bello." Her face pinkens between the orange flecks.

"Well, you just enjoy," Mom tells her. "Girls with your figures can eat whatever they want. Now, could I just have your mother's phone number?"

"Sure. This is her cell." Morgan holds out her own cracked phone for Mom to see the number.

Mom calls and seems happy with whatever Morgan's mom answers, just as Morgan predicted.

Meanwhile, I put out some fresh kibble and water for Diesel. He glances toward the two boxes on the counter. Then he gives me a long mournful stare. *This is what I'm getting? Nothing better?*

You have too many treats. You need nutrition, too.

Kibble, bleah! He slowly shuffles to his dish, begrudgingly sniffs, and finally crunch-crunches through.

"I'll go get my things," I tell Morgan. Packing a towel, my toothbrush, some underwear, and a long T-shirt to sleep in, I'm ready in about five minutes. I pass Mom in the hall.

"You have fun, Naomi."

"Uh huh. We're going swimming with some friends later." Being totally truthful should make me feel less tense, but it doesn't. I throw my arms around her. "Love you," I tell her, 'cause you never know.

She squeezes back.

Still wearing the knock-'em-dead red underneath, I should feel strong as I head back to the kitchen to Morgan and Diesel. My underwater swim stroke might keep me alive in an emergency, after all. Money shouldn't be so tight when we move in with Aunt Cathie, and my parents just have to get back together, lizard man movie or not.

"You think the donuts will be all right in the heat? Maybe we should have one, just in case," Morgan suggests.

"In case what?" I ask, holding the two boxes away from her.

"You know, they melt or get smooshed, the cream drools out of them. Gimme that," she reaches for the box.

Me, too, I would like some. "Rawf!"

"Fine." I carefully open the top box. The donuts look like a party. I take a double chocolate and bite in. "Mmm, Mom bought fresh!"

"Wonders never cease." Morgan grabs a pink-iced sprinkle.

"Thought you wanted the sour-cream glaze," I say.

"Saving that one. Sprinkles are awesome as long as you can brush your teeth." She bites in and I can hear the crunch.

Sweet, tiny, coloured kibble! Both Diesel's ears lift and he quickly dives for the blue and yellow bits that rain on the floor.

When he's finished lapping them up, Morgan makes him do his balancing act again, this time with a donut bit on his muzzle. "Wait, wait!" She holds up a finger and counts.

Look at me. What I don't do to amuse you humans!

"One, two, … and go!"

Diesel lifts his head, sends the piece of donut into the air, and then snaps it up.

"You're such a good dog!" She pats Diesel.

Oh, you have no idea! He turns and licks her.

She hugs him. "King used to do that trick all the time." Morgan's mouth twists.

"Thanks for giving Diesel his collar," I tell her. My dog is alive; hers is not. Even Diesel feels sad for Morgan. He licks her face and I hug both of them at the same time.

"Okay, well, let's go," Morgan says, and we break apart and head out.

The heat nearly knocks me over as we step out the door, but Morgan's house is only a couple of blocks away. "Hot enough to fry an egg," I complain. "Think I'm going to melt."

"Who cares?" Morgan says. "'Long as the donuts don't." She happily carries the two boxes and Diesel's leash. "We're here already."

Her house looks identical to ours, a two-bedroom town-house like most of the houses in the neighbourhood, only her mom hasn't decorated the kitchen as pretty. The cupboards are dark and the walls are bandage-coloured. We put the donut boxes on the counter, and a tall, toothy boy with large freckles comes running in.

"Rawf!" Diesel wags at him.

"Hey, doggie!" Morgan's brother bends down and wraps his arms around Diesel. I watch him and think it must be nice to have a younger brother, not so little as Luanne, someone you can actually talk to. He looks up and sees what's on the counter. "Can I have one?"

"Wait till after supper, Kieran," Morgan answers.

"I'm starving now." He still holds on to Diesel, who laps at his face frantically, as though he wants to be freed. "When do we eat?"

"In another hour. Let the dog go now."

Kieran drops his arms.

Morgan whistles and Diesel follows us downstairs to the bedroom she shares with her sister. A brother and a sister, I sigh. She's lucky. The room spans almost the entire basement, what would be our theatre room. Huge. Like a girl cave. The walls are covered in Wonder Woman posters. The two beds have blue duvets with large silver monograms, *M* for Morgan and *R* for Rachael. The *R* one looks neatly made, the corners even, but the *M* one looks crumpled, like someone just got out of it. Diesel crawls under that one.

"Hey, Rachael's gonna be late today because of extra band practice. Let's do manis and pedis." She crosses over to the neater side of the room and grabs some nail polish and other equipment. "Look, she has some decals we can use. You think they'll stay on when we're swimming?" She frowns at the tiny package.

"Won't she mind us using her stuff?"

"She'll never know. We'll be long gone before she even gets home. Hey, look at these. Little red roses. If you use the white polish, they'll really pop."

For sure Rachael will notice twenty missing nail decals. Still, those flowers would go perfectly with my bathing suit. And likely she'll blow up at Morgan, not me. "Let's do it," I agree.

"All right!" Morgan brings a box of tissues over, and we rip and crumple bits to squeeze between our toes. Morgan opens the nail polish.

Diesel pants. *Pew! That is stinky!*

First Morgan paints my nails. Then she sticks the roses on, slightly off-centre.

"They're crooked," I complain. Just like Morgan. She's always doing stuff that's just slightly not right, like using her sister's stuff right now.

She unsticks the one on my big toe and centres it. "Okay, Miss Fussy Pants?"

"Perfect."

One by one she straightens the flowers and paints over them with clear polish. When she finishes, I paint her toenails orange and stick some sparkly butterflies on them. Morgan paints her fingernails as I lacquer over the butterflies.

"I guess you learned all about makeup and stuff from your sister," I say.

"Are you kidding? She's such a witch. She kicks me out of my own room when she's getting ready to go out." Morgan places a sparkly butterfly in the bottom corner of one thumb. "Does that look good there?"

"No, place it dead centre." I stick a rose on my index finger. "Are you putting them on every nail?"

"Of course! It's a special night."

I raise an eyebrow as I keep sticking. Maybe we're pinning too much on this swim party.

For each finger I have a new thought. The thumb: What if those girls only hang around so they can make fun of us? The pointer finger: Supposing Dad doesn't show for movie night because of my red bikini? The middle finger: Or Mom really does hate *The Shape of Water*? The ring finger: What if they never get back together? The pinky: What if I die like before and never get to go to high school at all, never mind hang out with these girls?

Wait, was that a door slamming? Who is that stomping across the floor upstairs?

Tuesday, June 29:

Lies Between Sisters

Diesel's head peeks out from under the bed, blue duvet draped over his shoulders. He gives a small woof. *Alert, someone coming.*

"Morgan, get out of the room. I want to take a shower."

"Oh my gawd. It's Rachael," Morgan hisses. "Just a minute," she calls back. "We're changing!" She tosses me the clear polish. "Quick, varnish over them." She begins ripping the tissue from between her toes. Then she rips the tissue from mine. "We have to hide our toes or she's gonna notice them." She pulls some socks from a drawer and passes me a pair.

"I'm really hot! Will ya hurry up?" Rachael yells.

"Rawf!" *Running!* The more we rush around, the more excited Diesel becomes, jumping and wagging his tail. It seems like such a fun game to him.

"Was this how it looked before?" I ask after I reshelve Rachael's nail gear.

"Absolutely." Morgan doesn't even look over. "Let's get out of here." Diesel pushes ahead up the stairs.

"What a nice doggie," Rachael coos to him as he scrambles to the top. She scowls at Morgan, coming up next. "Your turn to make supper and you haven't even started." She wrinkles her nose and sniffs. That nail polish smell. But she doesn't say anything.

"I'm coming up to make it right now!" Morgan shoves her sister away from the door.

Rachael stands to the side to let me pass. Dressed in a blue-grey air force uniform and clunky black shoes, she looks cranky and sweaty, her blond hair escaping from a bun tucked into the back of a hat. In her arms she holds a large oddly shaped black case.

"Whoa. She's scary," I say after she shuts the door behind us.

"Band practice never puts Rachael in a good mood." Morgan shrugs, then takes some meatballs out from the freezer and puts them in the microwave.

"Can I do something to help?"

"Set the table. Cutlery is in that drawer."

I place the forks and knives on the table. Morgan puts some water on to boil and opens a couple of cans of tomato sauce.

"Can you wash this?" She tosses me a bag of lettuce from the fridge. "Here's the colander." As she stands up, we both notice the open box of donuts.

She sighs. "Kieran ate some." She turns back to watch the water on the stove, a bag of angel hair pasta in her hand.

"So what? That's not a big deal, is it?"

Morgan shrugs. A bubble pops in the water and she dumps the pasta in. "Pass me the meatballs from the microwave."

I do and she dumps them into the sauce on the stove.

"Why did your sister join the air force if she doesn't like practice?" I ask.

"Air cadets. She joined because she wants to learn how to fly, not play the tuba." After about ten minutes, Morgan flings a noodle at the wall and it sticks. "Kieran!" she calls.

He runs in, jam bleeding from the corners of his mouth.

Morgan scoops some pasta onto a plate and tops it with sauce and a couple of meatballs. "Here, take your plate," she says as she hands it to him. She fills three more and we take those to the table and sit down.

Then Rachael bursts into the kitchen dressed in shorts and a T-shirt, her long hair in a damp ponytail. "Did you take my straightener?"

"Um, no."

That little hesitation — my guess is she's lying.

"Where is it, then?" Rachael snaps.

"Check in Mom's bathroom. Maybe she used it. Your dinner's right here on the table." Her smile leans crookedly as she points to the plate across from her. That smile makes her look guilty.

Rachael slides into the chair next to me. I tuck my fingers around the fork and spoon to hide my nails.

"Kieran, will you stop playing with your food and start eating?" Rachael scolds.

"You're not the boss of me."

I notice him slip a meatball down to Diesel, but I don't say anything so he won't get in trouble.

"Have some salad at least," Rachael tells him.

He just picks at the pasta.

"You love angel hair. Come on, Kieran. Eat something." Suddenly, Rachael's eyes narrow. "What's that white stuff on your chin?"

He quickly wipes.

"You let him have donuts before dinner," she says to Morgan. Morgan doesn't have time to answer. "Of all the stupid things —"

"He only had one," Morgan says. "Eat up, Kieran. It's yummy."

"Nobody's going to make you anything else later," Rachael crabs at him. She softens her tone as she turns to me. "You're Naomi, right?" She nods by way of hello. "Nice nails. I bought some of those flowers myself."

"Thanks." I try to hide them around the fork again. Too late, really.

"Who wants more meatballs?" Morgan asks cheerily.

"Hey!" Rachael points at Morgan's hands. "You've got

butterflies on your nails." Dead quiet as all the synapses click inside Rachael's head. The quiet before a volcano blows. "Those are my decals, aren't they?" No answer. "Well, aren't they?" she thunders.

Morgan still doesn't answer.

Rachael's face turns fiery. "You took the straightener, too, didn't you?"

Morgan just smiles. I feel her sister's irritation under my own skin. Understand it, really. Nobody has to answer her; the truth is in Morgan's smile.

"You cow."

"Rawf!" Diesel jumps up.

Gunshot quick, Rachael zings a meatball at Morgan's head.

Morgan ducks.

The meat is loose! Diesel scuttles after the projectile.

"Go, Diesel!" Kieran calls.

Anticipating the moment Morgan's head will come back, Rachael launches another one.

It hits Kieran's cheek and bounces off. "Ow!"

Diesel abandons the meatball on the floor and snaps this one before it lands. Beautiful catch!

"Wow." Rachael stops her hand in mid-throw of a third one. "That dog is amazing."

"What did he do?" a woman's voice asks. I look up from the dog and see Morgan's mother standing in the doorway of the kitchen, a couple of bags of groceries in each hand. Tall and pale like Morgan, only with wrinkles instead of freckles, she watches us with similar grey eyes. She walks over to the counter and sets the bags down, wiping at her forehead. "And why are you eating with your hands, Rachael?"

"Oh me? I wasn't. I was just throwing this for the dog. He's as good as King. Check it out." She flings her last meatball hard, past Morgan's ear, and once again Diesel makes an astonishing leap for it.

Her mother folds her arms across her chest and shakes her head. My mom would have yelled about wasting food or maybe about throwing it around and making a mess. Some sauce has splashed on the wall behind Diesel. Instead, Morgan's mom smiles. "He really is amazing. Rachael, would you put these groceries away, please? I want to take a shower."

Morgan leaps up. "I'll do it!" She heads to the counter as her mother leaves the room.

"When I tell her you stole my stuff again, you'll be grounded for a month," Rachael grumbles.

"You threw meatballs at me. You'll be grounded, too." Morgan smiles as she loads some ice cream into the freezer. "Cookie dough, my favourite. That's because Mom likes me best."

Rachael zings one of Kieran's meatballs at Morgan. This one hits, then drops into Morgan's hand.

Give it to me! Diesel leaps up.

"Ow, ow, ow! I'm going to have a bruise. Naomi, check my face. Do you see a mark?"

I shrug my shoulders, not wanting to join this war.

"Fine. I won't tell Mom about the nail decals."

"Here, Diesel, catch!" Morgan pitches the last missile, and Diesel snaps it from the air just like before. Morgan continues to put the groceries away, finishing just as her mother walks in.

She rubs a towel over her hair. "You left your straightener in my bathroom, Rachael."

"Maybe Morgan wants to borrow it," Rachael says with an edge in her voice.

"Thanks anyway," Morgan answers. "But we're going swimming. My hair will only get all wet."

"Where?" her mom asks.

"You know, the place Uncle Lurch looks after over on Castlefield? We'll be there with a couple of other friends."

"You watch out for each other. And be back by eleven."

Morgan nods. "For sure."

Her mother tastes a forkful of angel hair from the pot. "Mmm. *Al dente*, just the way I like it. You girls go on. Rachael and Kieran can clean up."

We head out quickly before Rachael can complain. Diesel trots neatly at Morgan's side.

"I'm surprised my sister didn't kill me," Morgan tells me as we head for the terrific pool on the other side of town. "Gonna be a great night."

I nod. For once, though, I feel lucky not to have any brothers and sisters.

20

Tuesday, June 29:

Pool Party

Sitting on the cement deck at the side of the pool, we both watch the latch on the gate.

"Is my hair all right?" I ask. Frizzy as always, it just sproings back when I pat it.

The gate doesn't budge.

"Your hair has its own look, you know?" Morgan flicks her own long hair back.

Diesel paces, looking from Morgan to me. *Swimming?*

"When are they going to get here?" I ask Morgan, looking up at the grey sky. Must be seven thirty, but it's no cooler and the sun won't set till nine. There's not a spit of a breeze — not even a fern waves. The air feels heavy, and sweat trickles down my back. "Looks like it might storm. Maybe they won't come."

"Any minute, they'll be here."

We sit on our towels, arranging and rearranging our legs, trying to look relaxed and graceful. I want to bite my nails, I'm so nervous. I raise my fingers to my mouth and then see the flowers on them and smile instead. *I look great*, I tell myself. *I can almost swim, at least underwater, and my dog's alive. My parents are together, even if it's only for a couple of hours.*

Any food? Diesel strolls over, sniffs, and then licks at my palm. *Salty. Yum.*

"Do you want to go in for a swim?" Morgan asks.

"Do I ever. But I don't want to look like a drowned mouse when those girls get here."

"Don't dive under. Just glide over the top."

Easy for her to say. I haven't mastered floating yet. Still, I don't want to sweat, either. Maybe now is the time to try. I jump to my feet and step down the pool stairs. Morgan follows.

Me first for safety. Diesel pushes past me and begins circling through the water. I walk slowly. Three steps, four. Ahh! The water reaches my waist, only mid-thigh on Morgan.

"Hello?" a voice calls from the other side of the gate.

"Rawf!" Diesel barks hello back.

"Just lift the latch. It's not locked," Morgan calls.

I imagine those girls walking in to see me skimming gracefully through the water and jump in the rest of the way, sending my arms ahead in a breaststroke. At the same time, my legs kick back froggy-style. It feels good, cool, smooth.

Suddenly, a huge crash sends waves of water over me. I cough and reach my feet for the bottom so I can stand and breathe. Too deep. I sink down. *No, no!* I windmill my arms. My legs don't work in time with them. I want to scream, but nothing comes from my mouth except bubbles.

Diesel barks. *I'm here for you.* He swims next to me.

That makes me come out of my panic enough to realize, *Hey, I'm underwater now. I can definitely swim here.* I point myself toward the shallow end, swim one arm's length, and stand up.

Tom's flattened red hair surfaces first, then the rest of his head, his eyes, nose, and grin. He sputters water everywhere like some kind of seal. "Hi, Morgan. Naomi."

"What …" I splutter.

"Hi, Tom. Where's Simon?" Morgan asks.

"He'll be here in another five, with the others." Tom swims like he dives, loud and splashy.

"Simon?" I repeat.

"Wouldn't be a party without him. Am I right?" She winks.

"You said this was just a get-together with friends," I say to Morgan.

"Don't worry," Tom says. "No one posted it on the internet. It's just us and a few girls."

That's why the cool girls are coming. Not because we invited them to swim with us, but because Simon will be here. Still, Morgan says Simon likes me. They won't ignore me. Not if he pays attention to me. *Morgan says* ... but is she really 100 percent reliable or does she just need me along while she makes a play for Tom?

My dog's alive. I can swim underwater. Everything is okay, I tell myself as I start to breathe too quickly. But she lied to me. Put one over on me again. I kick my legs and dive under the water, where everything moves slow and blob-like and I can't help but feel relaxed. When I poke my head out again, I hear the latch click.

Checking, checking. Diesel climbs the pool stairs quickly and heads to the gate.

Then some voices:

"Oh my gawd. I can't believe we get to swim here."

"Like, who lives here, a movie star?"

Lots of giggles and then the gate bursts open. It's the fabulous four, the tall girls, the cool girls.

"Hi there!" Tara, the tousle-haired brunette, waves at me.

Diesel, the traitor, wags his butt off, swivelling from one to the other.

"Who's a cute puppy wuppy?" Francesca, the black-haired, chisel-cheeked girl, asks as she pats him.

"Ew, what's that smell? Is there a skunk nearby?" Brenna fans her hand in front of her nose.

"Hi," Morgan calls, breaking into her usual wonky grin.

I glare at her. She is just the perfect hostess.

"Hi, Peanut," Simon calls.

He still doesn't call me by my real name. Should I bother getting out of the water? Those girls' legs are taller than I am. I push my hands along the edge and hoist myself up awkwardly. I crawl to my feet, feeling foolish.

Brenna points. "Elevator girl. You're the brainy girl who tutors, right?"

"The little genius kid!" Tara chimes in.

"I wouldn't call her a genius," Morgan says. Strange, but it feels like she's trying to defend me.

"She's the kid who tutored you, isn't she?" Brenna asks.

Morgan told everyone about that? What else did she tell them?

She opens her mouth to say something, but Simon beats her to it. He gestures with his palm up toward me. "Ladies, allow me to introduce you to Pea—"

"Naomi," Morgan finishes for him. "Her name is Naomi."

I stand, dripping, on the other side of the pool, wishing I had something cute and funny to say. Even the shortest of the girls, Su-Ling, who truly has the best skin of all of them, towers over me. Still, I like her best, the only one I don't really want to kill at this moment.

"Is this your house?" Su-Ling asks me as she pulls a can of pop from out of her bag.

"No, a friend of Morgan's uncle owns it." As I speak I see movement up at the second-floor window next door. A blind slat lifts up and the apple-doll face looks out.

I raise my hand to my head in a salute but she frowns and pulls away.

Simon tugs off his jeans. Underneath, he wears orange board shorts with a lightning bolt on them. He pulls off his T-shirt and I look away.

"What are you waiting for, ladies?"

The girls giggle and peel off their own skirts and tops till they're all standing in stringier bikinis than mine. But, of course, their bodies … not so stringy.

I walk over to our towels, pick up a box of donut bits, and pop it open in front of Simon. "Would you like a sour-cream glaze?" I ask.

"Hey, yeah, thanks. Right after my swim." He takes two long steps and jackknifes into the pool. Tara and Francesca inch their way down the stairs.

"Oooh, it's cold." Tara folds her arms across her chest and scrunches her shoulders.

Brenna cannonballs like Tom.

Su-Ling helps herself to a donut bit. "My favourite," she tells me. "Here, take a pop, if you like."

"I shouldn't. There's no bathroom, you know." But I pick out a raspberry fizz and pull the tab as I sit down on the towel. Diesel immediately flops down next to me.

Su-Ling waves her hand. "Doesn't matter. You just go in the water. Everyone does it."

Ew. I grab a couple of donut bits and Diesel's tail waves up a storm. "You want one, you have to work for it," I tell him. "Roll over, roll over. All the way. That's it!"

"Such a well-trained dog." Su-Ling pulls out a portable speaker from her bag, connects it to her phone, and swipes the volume up. "Too bad he smells so bad."

Now I want to kill her, too.

Simon likes me, I tell myself. What can I do to start a conversation with him? I throw a bit of donut up high and Diesel leaps and snaps it in his jaws. Beautiful. Couldn't have done it better. Simon dives under the water at the same time, though, and misses it.

"My favourite song!" Su-Ling stands and starts to wiggle to her music. Simon surfaces again. Her dance definitely catches his attention.

"Come on in. The water's fine."

He isn't inviting me — he's asking her, and they're all ignoring me. Middle school all over again. I pop another donut into my mouth, swig back some raspberry fizz, and belch. "Oops, excuse me," I tell no one in particular.

Such a large growl from a small human. Diesel tilts his head in wonderment. *Nice!* He opens his mouth and gives a grinning pant.

Tom and Morgan start a splash war. They aren't fooling anyone; they are sooo flirting. Fine, she's getting the guy she wants. That's what this is all about.

I feel my face get hotter. I drink some more pop, feel anxious and desperate, then breathe in deeply, trying to relax. The music seems to grow louder. I stand up, and Diesel jumps to his paws. Maybe I *will* dance. I shuffle my feet a little to the music. I give a bit of a shimmy. It feels weird to be dancing on the pool deck all by myself.

So I climb down the stairs into the pool, Diesel nudging my back with his moist nose. With seven people already in, water splashes at me from every angle.

Whoosh! Simon keeps lifting Su-Ling up and throwing her back in. Her hair is plastered to her head. She blinks the water from her eyes and shoves at his chest in protest.

I would take that crash into the water and having my hair get wet and frizz up even more if it meant even ten seconds of that kind of attention. A loud, metallic song blasts from Su-Ling's speaker, and I dance to it as I drift closer to Simon. I swivel my hips as hard as I can without breaking them. But it's too late.

He stares into her eyes as he lifts out of the water. For a moment it seems like he will kiss her.

I sink down, down, into the water. No hope for me. Everyone looks as though they are part of a music video or a soft-drink commercial, jumping, splashing, shrieking, laughing. *I like being a loner*, I remind myself.

I love you. Diesel's nose drifts close to my face and he licks at my cheek. *You are my favourite person.*

Really, my only best friend is a dog.

I suddenly have to get away. I flounder back to the stairs and climb out. Slip on my flip-flops, throw on my top, grab my towel, and creep around to the back of the shed. I think if I can take a few breaths on my own, I will be able to make it through the night.

No one seems to notice. Diesel runs around me and barks, which might have attracted everyone's attention, but then he spots his favourite digging hole and focuses on it. The sod flies up. I check that second-floor window, but apple doll isn't here.

"Rawf!" *Danger.*

I listen. Over the noise of the pool I hear car doors slam.

"Police!" Morgan says.

Then a deep voice comes from the other side of the house. Not one I recognize.

"Good evening. There's been a complaint from the neighbours."

21

Tuesday, June 29:

Wrong Place, Wrong Time

Apple doll's face suddenly appears at that top window, grinning at me. She nods and points to me. "Over here!"

Oh great, she's telling the cops where I am. But I'm lip reading. They can't really hear her from wherever they are now. I can still make my getaway.

Diesel continues to fling dirt from his hole, so I drop down next to him and push. "Go under, boy, go!" I shove at his haunches, and in another moment he's on the other side. Then I stuff my towel through. My turn. But for once, I'm too big for something. Instead I climb. One foot goes into the bottom rung of the fence, then I reach for the top crossbar and hoist myself up so that my thigh clears the top.

Officers! Hurry! Over there! Those words I'm just imagining. I can't know for sure what apple doll's lips are saying. But she's rapping on the window now.

My other leg follows the first, but a fence prong digs along the bottom of my thigh. That will be a bruise. When I hit the ground, I roll.

"Let's get out of here, boy!"

That's when I realize his leash still lies back near the box of donuts, along with the rest of my clothes. Can I just make a quick grab for his collar whenever a bus or motorcycle passes? No, I can't take the chance. I look up.

"Officers!" I see her lips move.

Quickly, I tear a strip from my old cereal towel, roll it, and loop it under Diesel's collar. Doubled up, the towel makes a very short leash that I think can hold.

"Come on, boy." I slap my thigh and he trots neatly beside me. Perfect, no strain to the towel at all.

As we rush out of the neighbour's yard, I look back to see the apple-doll lady shaking her fist.

Too bad for her. So good for us.

"Woof!" *What about Wiener Girl?*

"Never mind her," I tell him as we walk quickly away from the police car. It's twilight now and no buses or cars pass us. So quiet, it gives me time to think. We can go straight home, and I can tell Mom that Morgan and I had a fight. She won't know about our little party, including boys, at a pool that doesn't even belong to us. Morgan can bring the rest of my stuff later. If she doesn't land in jail or get grounded.

Not that I ever want to see her again. She likes Diesel fine, but me, that has to be faking. Simon didn't talk to me all evening, didn't even try my donuts. And I can't blame him, really. How could he pay attention to me with all those beautiful, tall girls hanging around him? It's Morgan I blame for not telling me the guys were coming. For lying about Simon liking me. Some big joke on Peanut, the little genius kid, all so Morgan can make her play for Tom.

Diesel hesitates at the corner and looks back toward the house with the pool. He sits down, one ear up, one down, then turns his head to the side and whimpers at me. *Wiener Girl?*

"She won't get in trouble like I will," I tell him. "Bet her mother won't care that boys were there."

Diesel woofs gently and I hold tight to the towel ends as we cross the street together. Another block and then another. At each corner he sits pretty for me, and in between he walks nicely at my heels.

The sky darkens gradually. I can't believe I ever thought Morgan was my friend. Although I have to admit, Diesel behaves beautifully now and she helped me train him. Maybe she only hangs with me because of my dog and because she misses King. She always lies to everyone. My eyes burn. I shake my head.

Diesel shakes his head, too. *You are wrong about Wiener Girl.*

He suddenly stops dead, fur along his backbone rising. Too late, I see what sits on the lawn across the street, motionless, ears stiff and tall. A large brown rabbit. For a moment or two the bunny and Diesel stare at each other. Neither seems to believe their luck.

Then the rabbit springs across the lawn, poufy white tail taunting from the rear.

I hear the towel tear, and I grab for Diesel's collar.

"No!" I cry out. My fingernails bend backward. I can't hold on. Diesel bolts.

He should be all right. Not a car or motorcycle has passed us all night. This isn't even a bus route. Then, like in some kind of nightmare, a red Smart Car appears out of nowhere. Could it be the car from my hallucination? *Déjà vu* or *déjà vécu*, whatever. Is there just no way to avoid Diesel's fate?

The car doesn't brake or swerve off its path. It just speeds toward him.

"Stop!" I scream, holding my face in my hands. But like a car possessed, it continues relentlessly.

Then I hear the thump and Diesel's body rolls away. I scream, but nothing comes from my lips.

"Diesel!" Morgan runs up beside me. "I saw the Smart Car! Your dream was right." Where did she come from? I want to yell at her that this is all her fault, but she doesn't stop; she just continues onto the road. "Poor, poor doggie," she coos as she kneels down beside him.

"Is he …?" I say the word in my head and my lips move, but I don't know if any sound actually comes out.

"He's still breathing. We have to get him off the street. Help me."

I run out beside her. My eyes blur as I watch him struggle to get up. It's as if the back part of his body doesn't work anymore.

Ow, ow, ow. My haunches hurt!

"Shh, boy. Easy!" Morgan keeps him down with one hand on his neck. The other pulls a towel from her bag. "Help me spread this out."

I can't move. My chest starts heaving, but I can't get any air.

"Snap out of it. Diesel needs you."

Numb, I take the ends and pull them straight.

"On three we're going to lift together to get him on the towel. You take his shoulders. One … two … three. Gentle."

Diesel looks me in the eyes. *Don't tell Alpha Female!*

Don't tell Mom? "I failed you. I'm sorry."

"Nobody's failing anyone." Morgan's arm suddenly lifts up like a train crossing signal, her hand pointing. "Look over there! There's that cop car again. I'm going to flag him down." Morgan runs toward it, waving and yelling.

My heart stops beating. Is she crazy? What if the police officer can't see her and doesn't stop in time? Everything can turn so much worse. The car swivels. The brakes squeal. The door flings open.

My heart flip-flops into life again.

"Officer Forsyth, can you help my friend's dog? He's been hit by a car." Blah, blah, blah, more talking I can't listen to or process. I feel like I'm dying inside my dog. The officer steps out and opens the back door. Then he walks over and slips his arms beneath the towel. Diesel's head and legs flop over, his eyes still locked on to mine.

The floppiness scares me. "Please, please, be all right," I beg him.

I am so tired.

Officer Forsyth loads Diesel onto the back seat and I squeeze in beside him. Diesel lifts his head and rests it on my thigh. Morgan squishes into the back seat with us. I can feel Diesel's breath hot on my leg, and feel grateful for what that means. "Diesel," I whisper and gently pat his head.

The police officer talks into his radio, telling them about his animal-hospital run. I'm on the edge of the seat thinking he will be ordered not to help us. But instead he turns on the siren and we pull away.

I bend down, close to Diesel's ears. "I can't do this without you," I whisper.

He turns his head and licks my face. I kiss his whiskers back.

Five blocks north, ten blocks west — after the longest ten-minute ride of my life, the squad car finally pulls up to the front of an emergency animal hospital. Officer Forsyth springs out, lifts Diesel off me, and carries him across the lot. In the lead, Morgan rushes to open the door to the building. I keep my eyes on Diesel's, hoping I will hold on to his life that way.

Brightly lit and painted yellow, the waiting room smells like cough medicine and a million scared cats. When the receptionist sees us, she stands up and calls out to someone in the back. "This way," she says to us as she flings open a door to a small, kitchen-like room with a stainless-steel examining table in the middle. Officer Forsyth lays Diesel down on the metal table, which ordinarily would freak him out, but he still has Morgan's towel between him and that cold shininess.

I'm here for you, Diesel.

"You girls will contact your parents, right?" the officer asks as he straightens. "I need to head out."

Morgan nods.

"Good luck." Officer Forsyth touches his hat with his hand.

It only registers then that he means goodbye.

Don't call Alpha Female!

"Why not, Diesel? Why not?" I ask out loud.

I will get the sleeping needle.

How do you know that? What really happened last time?

He won't answer. It doesn't matter. Diesel's right. My parents can't afford any kind of vet bills. Mom will have him put down.

A tall woman with a brown ponytail and a white lab coat rushes in. Dr. Fielding, her name tag reads. "You girls need to take a seat out in the reception area. I'll come out to talk to you as soon as I know more."

We do as she asks. I begin shaking.

"You probably want to put these on," Morgan says, tossing me my clothes from her bag.

I slip on my shorts, wishing I had a sweater. My teeth are still chattering.

"Wanna borrow this?" She hands me a sweatshirt from her bag.

"Thanks." I put it on.

"You want to call your mom?" Morgan holds out her cellphone.

"I can't. If Diesel needs any kind of treatment, she'll tell the doctor to put him down."

"You don't know that."

Oh, but Diesel knows. He told me as much. "We don't have any money, Morgan. We're moving in with my aunt at the end of the month."

"You have your babysitting money."

"And I have money in the bank, too. But I don't think she'll let me spend it on saving Diesel." I shake my head. "And I can't take the chance."

"I can call my mom," Morgan suggests.

"Won't she just tell my mother?" I ask.

"You have a point." Morgan frowns, then taps her nose. "There's something else we can try, someone else who should take responsibility. But we'll have to stall the vet for time. Probably till tomorrow at the least. Do you think you can do that?"

22

Tuesday, June 29:

Consequences

"We don't know if Dr. Fielding can even help Diesel yet." I stare down at the speckled tile, so flat and boring and yet somehow able to retain the cat smell. I want to gnaw at my nails, but once again the flower decals stop me. "She's taking a long time."

"That's a good sign. With King she came out right away and said we needed to put him down."

"I don't know." I look up from my hands to the wall. A sad-looking puppy stares out from a poster there. *Only you can save your pet from heartworm.*

"Why did you take off like that anyway? Without Diesel's leash, even."

"The cops came." That makes me sound like such a suck. "It's not like I really belonged anyway." I stare at the heartworm poster and the message seems to change: *Only you can save your dog from getting hit by a car.* Those brown puppy eyes accuse me, just as Morgan's questions do. If I had waited around with her through the police interrogation, I would have had Diesel's leash. Maybe we would have missed the rabbit entirely or, if he had still been there and if Diesel had yanked the leash out of my hand, maybe that Smart Car might have been long gone already. I regret so hard, but it doesn't change anything.

"You belonged more than anyone else. You're the only one who's my real friend," Morgan says.

"Oh, come on. It wasn't your house. We were having a party at someone else's pool."

"Officer Forsyth understood. I explained about Uncle Lurch letting us have people over. All we had to do was turn the music down."

"You asked your uncle for permission?" I turn to look at Morgan.

"Well, sure. Do you think I want to get in trouble with him?"

I picture the large, hairy biker dude and shake my head.

"Then after Officer Forsyth left, we saw you were missing. I was worried. So I sent everyone home and went looking for you."

"I felt like such a geek. The little genius kid who tutored you."

"You are a geek! Must be nice to be so smart."

"Everyone ignored me."

"I was making my big play for Tom. Thanks for ruining that," Morgan says. "You were supposed to be chatting up Simon! Remember our plan to have boyfriends in high school?"

"That was never my plan. Besides, he only paid attention to Su-Ling. Those girls are all so gorgeous."

"They just know how to distract him. You're smart and beautiful. You have to —"

I stop listening to Morgan and stand up as Dr. Fielding comes into the reception area.

"Is, is … he okay?" I ask.

She smiles and nods. "He's a very lucky dog. We stabilized him. His vital signs are good. He may have a small fracture in the pelvic area. We'll need to take X-rays to see. Did you call your parents?"

"We couldn't reach them. But it's all right — I can pay for this. I have money in my bank account."

"Well, he's resting comfortably now. I'd like to keep him overnight in any case for observation. If your parents are good with it, you can fill out the forms for … Diesel, is it?"

I nod.

"And they can sign when they come in."

"Thank you so much!" I clasp my hands together. Morgan has the overnight delay she wants. "Um, do you have an idea of how much this will cost?"

"Stabilization comes to eight hundred. With the overnight stay, X-rays, and any treatment, I'm afraid we're looking at just under two thousand."

I gulp. It will wipe everything out of my account, all my babysitting money, and I'll have to borrow another twenty dollars. Still. I can do this, and if I can save Diesel, maybe this summer can turn out all right after all. "Thanks again. I'm so happy you could help my dog."

She smiles. "It's what we're here for." She waves and then heads back into the office behind the reception desk.

"Hurry up with the form," Morgan hisses at me. "We want to get going as quickly as possible."

I zip through the questions. My name, his name, his age, our address and phone number. Pet insurance: none. His breed. I begin to slow down. *T. Rex*, I can hear Morgan saying, but I write down *Australian cattle dog*. Weight … oh, around fifty pounds. Is he neutered? Yes. Shots, yes, but I don't know the dates. Then I turn the clipboard in to the receptionist.

"What now?" I ask Morgan. "Do you know the bus routes for this area?"

"No. Let's take a cab. If I'm right about this, the clock could be ticking."

Confused, I squint at her a moment. "Where exactly are we going?"

"Westdale Avenue. I never told you, but I found that Smart Car we saw at the park there. It may have a dent or some of Diesel's DNA on the bumper. We're going to confront the driver."

"Do you think that's a good idea? What if he's violent?"

"It's a she. Do you have a better idea?"

I shake my head.

"I'll get us a cab." Morgan speaks into her phone, then turns back to me. "On its way."

"See you tomorrow," I tell the receptionist as we head for the door.

"Bye. And don't worry about your dog. We'll take good care of him."

We head outside to wait for our cab. The heat has died down to a gentle warmth, and the full moon lights up a clear sky full of twinkling stars. No Dog Star anywhere. What time is it anyway? Still *THU July 01 4:30* by my watch, of course. But it has to be close to ten now. We rush to the cab as it pulls up.

"Where to?"

"Um, um. Westdale Avenue." The driver looks at us suspiciously when Morgan can't give him an exact address. "I'm sorry. The house has white pillars in the front with ivy growing on the walls. Could be 2638 or 2338. I'll know it when I see it."

"You have the money?" the driver asks.

"Oh, for sure." Morgan waves a twenty-dollar bill in the air.

The driver growls something but punches an address into his GPS. We take off. What if the driver of the Smart Car hasn't gone home, maybe headed out of town instead? She seemed in an awful hurry or she would have stopped in time to save Diesel.

"Could you just cruise down the street slowly?" Morgan asks the driver as we turn onto Westdale. The large oak trees form a canopy overhead.

"Sure. Why not?" he growls. "Got nothing better to do." The cab creeps by the houses.

"That's it!" Morgan whispers. "It's there!" she shouts when the red Smart Car becomes visible in the driveway just beyond a tall hedge. The house has a triple garage, but the driver hasn't parked it indoors.

"Thank you. Keep the change." Morgan hands the driver that twenty and a five, which only gives him a dollar tip.

He growls again and drives away.

"I'll pay you back," I whisper. "What are we going to say?" I ask as we draw closer to the Smart Car.

"Look over here!" Morgan points to the passenger-side headlight, which is shattered. She takes a pencil and paper out of her bag and writes down the licence plate number. Then we head up the walkway.

The doorbell plays the first bar of Beethoven's Fifth Symphony. Scary sounding. Morgan and I look at each other. I press the button a second time just to hear it again. Morgan makes fists. Beethoven's Fifth stokes her!

A friendly-looking round lady with rimless glasses answers the door. "You girls are canvassing awfully late," she tells us. "What are you raising money for?"

"Miss, there was a hit and run about an hour ago involving your Smart Car. I have the licence number and we should go to the police, but we thought we'd talk to the driver first."

Whoa! Morgan takes my breath away. I make myself a promise right then and there: I will never think of Morgan as dumb or annoying again.

"Oh my god!" The woman puts her hand over her mouth. Then she drops it again and steps backward into the house. "Summer! Come down here immediately!"

She hasn't shut the door. It stays open wide, so Morgan and I step onto the white marble floor of her hallway. My eyes follow an oak staircase that winds up from the middle of it, past the chandelier and high hallway ceiling.

A slim girl in heels and jeans clatters down those stairs. She has bright blue eyes and smeared black mascara. A gold locket hangs from her neck.

"You were in an accident and drove away?" her mother calls.

"No!" She hesitates a moment. "I did hear a clunk under the car over on Broadway. Thought I'd hit a pothole."

"You never stopped to check," I say.

"I never saw anybody."

"You were going so fast, how could you?" Morgan says.

"We have your licence number."

"Did someone get hurt?" the friendly woman asks us.

"My dog." My mouth buckles. "He may have a broken pelvic bone."

"We want you to come to the animal hospital and sign for the bills," Morgan tells her, for once no smirk on her face.

I grab my chin with my hand so my mouth won't drop open in shock. I have to keep a poker face, too. We need them to do this. Diesel's life depends on it. I watch the mother, whose face looks pale but hard.

"I didn't know, Mom, honest! I thought I hit a pothole. I had a couple of drinks in Hess Village so I didn't stop."

Her mother shakes her head. "You'd risk not checking just to avoid a breath check?"

No answer. Then a shrug, some tears, and more mascara streaks down her cheek. "I'm sorry about your dog," Summer tells us.

"Could you maybe just drive a little slower from now on?" I ask.

"It's reckless driving is what it is," Morgan adds. "You could have hit Naomi. She was chasing Diesel."

It's true. She could have hit me; Diesel and I could have both been hurt. Or died. Like the last time through only a little different.

The mom continues to stare at Summer. "Of course we'll come to the animal hospital with you. Summer will sign and pay for all your dog's vet bills. It's only right."

Tuesday, June 29:

The Vet Bill

Both Summer and her mother seem to be animal lovers, so I actually believe she didn't know she'd hit Diesel. She's really sorry, too, and cries all the way over to the animal hospital.

But how bad a driver does that make her — not even noticing a dog's body rolling away in her rear-view mirror? And that Smart Car killed him last time, too, so I feel as though she's made the same mistake twice.

After Summer has given the animal hospital her credit card number, her mom drives us back to Morgan's house. The clock on her car dashboard shows eleven thirty, and the house seems quiet and dark except for the porch light. She walks us to the door, all the while looking around. For what? Signs of an adult, I bet — she doesn't seem comfortable just dropping us off. But I know I don't want to ring the bell, don't want to risk waking Morgan's mom, risk her getting my mother up, too.

"Um, here's my business card. Call me and let me know how Diesel's doing."

"We'll be okay. I've got my key," Morgan tells the lady as she unlocks the door and opens it a crack.

Finally, she heads back to her car and drives away, leaving me to stare at the creamy slip of cardboard. *Johnson and Peters, Attorneys at Law.* "She doesn't look like a lawyer." I flip the card to Morgan. "We're lucky she agreed to pay."

Morgan steps into the entrance and holds her finger to her lips. "Crazy lucky," she whispers. Morgan looks at the card, then up at me with a curled lip. "I still can't believe you left me behind at the swimming pool."

"You were busy with Tom. I was the one all by myself."

"But I brought Simon there for you!" She tiptoes through the hall ahead of me.

"He ignored me, just like you did," I whisper after her. "Tell the truth, he doesn't really like me."

She stops and turns around. "Exactly as I told you before. He thinks you're a hot pepper."

I raise my eyebrows. I don't think she said it exactly that way before.

"Honestly, guys like smart girls. That giggly dumb-girl thing those others do around him gets really old."

This coming from someone I used to think was dumb.

I shrug. "For you and me maybe. Simon seemed to like it just fine."

"Su-Ling started putting the moves on Simon back at the park pool when you backed away so you could learn to swim first. She just wore him down."

"You think Little Mermaid would have won him over?" I ask.

"No." She shakes her head. "Still, ya gotta learn to trust me, Naomi."

I think about that for a moment and nod. "Maybe you can help me with that."

"Apology accepted." She grins full out. "And just for the record, luck had nothing to do with getting Ms. Johnson to pay. We had them dead to rights. We make a great team, Naomi." She lifts her hand and we fist-bump. Then she flips on a light and we see her mother curled up asleep on the couch waiting for us.

She blinks sleepily and sits up. "What happened to you two? Where's Diesel?"

We explain everything, and it feels great to unload. I wish I could talk to Mom like this, but I don't know if she'd still stop Diesel's treatment. *Too much money. Doesn't matter who's paying it*, she might say. *You can feed a child in Somalia for years on that.*

"How awful! Are you okay?" She stands up and hugs me. She feels all bony, not soft and cozy like Mom. "You sure you don't want to go home. Or call your mother?"

"Thanks. I'm positive."

"Why don't you fix yourselves a snack and then head off to bed?" Morgan's mom suggests.

It surprises me just how hungry I suddenly become at the mention of a snack, so Morgan nukes us a couple of leftover sprinkle donuts.

"Did Simon get any treats?" I ask as she scoops vanilla ice cream into the centre of the donuts.

"Nope. I just shooed everyone out so I could hunt for you."

"I really did ruin everything. I'm sorry."

She just looks at me, then a smile creeps over her face and she waves her hand like it's all no big deal. Over and forgiven.

I chew at my lip as she hands me my plate, then change the subject. "You told me you get nightmares from eating too much sugar before bed."

"Yup, but I don't think they tell the future like *your* sugar nightmares."

"I don't remember eating anything sweet before that dream." I dig my spoon in.

"Anyhow, this donut is totally worth it." She grins with sprinkle-covered teeth. "And, if you do get a nightmare, just remember —"

"You've got my back?" I finish.

"No, I was going to say, I'll be right beside you. You can wake me."

We eat our little parties on plates and head downstairs, where we pile onto the messy bed with the silver *M* on the duvet. We don't talk since Morgan's sister lies snoring on the other one.

I need to toss and turn to work out what's happened to me and Diesel, but I don't want to move and accidentally touch Morgan. Instead I replay Diesel's voice in my head. That's what I most miss about him right now. I try to imagine him telling me that this will turn out all right.

But I still can't sleep. So no sugar nightmares tonight.

Wednesday, June 30:

The Nightmare

When the first bit of light filters through the small basement window, I jump out of bed and throw on my clothes. "Morgan." I gently shake her shoulder. "I have to go home."

"What, huh? What time is it? Let me get up. I'll go with you."

"No, it's too early. Go back to sleep. I'll call you as soon as I hear."

I run the few blocks to my house. I'm not a big jogger, so I can feel my heartbeat through my gums by the time I get there. I grab the phone from the kitchen and sneak into Mom's room to get that one, too. Don't want her answering the vet's call. I place them on my bed and lie down next to them, watching and listening.

The first time they ring, I startle awake and pick one up.

"I'm sorry but your dog died in surgery." No hello, no identification of the caller. I actually see the apple-doll lady smiling at me.

"But you didn't even take X-rays," I yell.

"Sure we did. Summer told us we could."

I scream then, loud and hard, and wake myself up for real this time. Stupid sprinkle donut and ice cream. Luckily, I don't wake Mom — must have screamed inside my head.

Next time the phone rings, I nearly don't wake up. I grab a receiver just as Mom walks into the room.

"Hello, Naomi?" the voice on the other end says.

"Yes."

"This is Dr. Fielding."

"How is Diesel?" I ask.

Mom watches, eyes wide and eyebrows in question mark.

"Well, he is doing just fine. He ate a big bowl of kibble this morning and he barked at the cat."

I smile, so relieved I need to swallow hard for a moment. Then I take a big breath. "What did the X-rays show?"

Mom's brows knit, and she digs her fists into her hips.

"No fracture, which is wonderful. But he scratched up his left hindquarter pretty badly, so he's sore. We bandaged it. You can pick him up whenever you are ready."

"Thanks so much, Dr. Fielding."

"You're welcome. Goodbye."

I put down the phone again and take another deep breath. I can't believe everything may still turn out okay.

"What happened to the dog?"

"Um, well, it's like this. We went for a walk and he saw a rabbit. When he chased it, he got hit by a car." I start slowly but then rush the rest of the words. "But he's okay. It was just a little car. The driver is paying for the vet bills."

"A little car?" Mom rubs her forehead with her fingertips.

"Yes, one of those Smart Cars."

She shakes her head. "Why didn't you call?"

"I didn't want to upset you." Her eyebrows question mark even higher, as though she isn't buying that explanation, so I take another breath and try the whole truth. "I thought you would tell the vet to put him down."

"If he was suffering …"

"Mom, the bill will be close to two thousand dollars."

Her head flies back as though someone socked her in the face.

"I would have paid the vet out of my own money," I say.

Horror opens Mom's eyes so wide they look like they will bug outside their sockets.

"But it's okay. Morgan helped me track down the driver."

"You mean he didn't stop?"

"It was a girl who didn't want her breath tested."

"Still, that was a dangerous thing for you to do." Mom shakes her head. Her eyes turn normal-sized again, but her head hangs down. "Alone."

"No, Mom. I had Morgan."

She lifts her chin and looks me in the eyes. Hers are shiny. "I only wish I could have helped you."

I take her arm. "Mom, you can help." I pause. "Is … is Dad here?"

"No. Why?"

The romantic night failed, too. I sigh. "Can you call him? We need to pick up Diesel now."

By *we*, I mean I hope she'll drive with us over to the hospital. But while the conversation on the phone sounds friendly enough, when Dad arrives the two of us head off without her.

"You know I love that dog myself," Dad says in the car. "I wish you would have told your mom and me what was happening."

"I wish I could have, too. It's just the money …"

"But it was so dangerous, going to the driver's house. I should have been there." He gives me a quick sideways glance and pats my knee. "We're broke right now, Naomi, there's no denying it. Lots of disadvantages. But I believe we can overcome most of our problems by using our imagination." He taps a finger against his head. Another sideways glance at me and a big smile. "The fact that you even thought of chasing after that driver proves you know how to overcome problems."

"Yeah, Dad, but that was Morgan's idea. And I would have told you what was happening if you lived at home." I trust him about Diesel. I know he loves him as much as I do.

"Your mom doesn't want me there anymore. She thought I kept Diesel skunky on purpose. Hated *The*

Shape of Water. Didn't like the way I packed the good dishes …"

"Do you really believe that? She was singing when you came over to help us pack the other day."

Dad frowns for a moment. "You've always been a smart girl. Do you still think I have a chance with your mother? Honestly?" He turns again to look at me for a second.

"I know you do."

"Huh." He turns back to watch the road, but the corners of his eyes crinkle. If Mom could only see the effect she has him, it would help win her over. She can't resist that smile, can she?

"Like you told me, you have to use your imagination. What does Mom like that doesn't cost anything? I know it makes her happy when I tell her I love her."

"Okay, Naomi. I have to think about this to come up with something, something romantic."

"Turn in over there, Dad. That's the entrance to the hospital."

He parks and we walk in together. "Pew, lots of cats must come through," Dad says.

"Let me get Diesel for you," the receptionist says when she sees me. "It will just be a few minutes. Have a seat."

We sit down beside each other.

"What about a picnic?" Dad says. "Tomorrow is July first. Your mother and I both have the day off."

Thursday! They didn't have the holiday off last time through. Things are moving differently. Hopefully that's a good sign.

"You would have to make the picnic. You can't just buy us fish and chips. Um, where would we go?"

"Hamilton Beach. Where we met. I'll make egg-salad sandwiches. She likes the way I make those. We can all have ice cream for dessert."

Hamilton Beach. Last time, it was Morgan who convinced me to go. For free ice cream. My heart drums hard against my chest. *Where I drowned.* "If you want romance, you don't need me around. Besides, I'll have to stay home and keep Diesel company."

"No. I want everybody there. I have things I want to tell you all."

"What about the bikini …" My voice trails off as Diesel limps out with Dr. Fielding. Around his neck he wears a large white satellite collar.

"Diesel!" I rush toward him so he won't bound over and hurt himself. I try to hug him, but his stiff plastic shield scratches my face.

He whines and swings his head this way and that. *I hate this thing around neck. I must get it off.*

"Poor, poor Diesel!" I pat his forehead. "Does he really have to keep the cone on?"

Dr. Fielding nods. "Sorry, but he just can't seem to leave that bandage alone," she says.

"How long does he have to wear the cone?" I ask as he scrapes it across my leg.

"This week at least. If you can keep him quiet, too, that would be best. Then you can bring him back in and we'll see."

Dad takes away some paperwork, but the bill is stamped *PAID IN FULL*. When we get back home, I take Diesel to my room and call Morgan. Dad talks to Mom in the kitchen. As Morgan and I chat on the phone, I cross my fingers that Dad's invitation will work.

"Diesel's fine," I tell her.

My back leg has a very itchy thing on it and I can't scratch.

You're so lucky! Don't complain. "It's like a miracle. But he needs to rest. I still have to watch Luanne today. Do you wanna come over?"

"You're inviting me to your house? Wow, is it my birthday or something?"

"What are you talking about? You come here all the time."

"Yeah, but you never invite me. Sure, I'll come. Be there in five."

When I hang up the phone, Dad is ready to leave. By the bounce in his step, I figure things went well with Mom.

"So did she like the picnic idea?"

"Yes. I told her I could come over early to help her pack as long as we could go for a picnic on the beach."

"Nice touch about the packing."

"She told me it was only right that I did my fair share." He smiles lopsidedly. "I guess she has a point."

"Dad, I have to tell you. I know you don't like my bikini but I can't wear Little Mermaid anymore."

He nods. "I am a little sad about that."

"Don't worry, Dad. I'm so little, none of the guys look at me."

"I think you're wrong about that, Naomi." He stoops to hold my chin in his hand. "You know both your mother and I will always love you, no matter what." He kisses my cheek. "Nothing that happens at any picnic will change that."

Of course I get that. But I want my family back together again. I check my watch — still flashing *THU July 01 4:30* — and I know the Thursday picnic can have the power to change everything.

Later that afternoon, Morgan brings Diesel some get-well presents: a bag of beef jerky and a previously enjoyed DVD, *Lassie*. Before we do anything else, Mom insists I pack all my closet for the big move, but Morgan helps me, so it goes fast. Together we fill four boxes and sort out a bag of clothes to donate to Goodwill.

Then I make popcorn, one of Diesel's other favourites, and we settle down to watch the movie. Diesel barks a few times at Lassie, but mostly he's interested in my popcorn. I throw him a couple but he misses them and they land in his cone. *More, more!* I pop one of the fallen ones in his mouth.

Morgan and I have seen the movie before — well, it's Diesel's present, after all — so we talk during some parts. I tell her about the picnic and how nervous I am about Dad trying to get back together with Mom.

"I wouldn't worry," she reassures me. "He's helping your mom with packing, making her food. If it doesn't work out, it just wasn't meant to be."

Meant to be. What does that even mean? That whatever fate decides is in store for us can't be changed? I refuse to believe that's true. Every choice and move we make has to shift the path of our life.

At the end of the movie, we both cry when Lassie tumbles over the waterfall, even though we know she will survive eventually.

I cry harder when I glance down at my watch and see tomorrow's date because I can feel myself sinking in the waves, too. But I take a deep breath. That four-thirty time can't mean anything to me because I won't drown, not if I don't go swimming and I'm not even planning to go near the water.

"Well, I better head home," Morgan says when the credits roll. "You're not going to invite me to the picnic tomorrow, are you?"

"Do you really want to be there when Dad makes his big play?"

"Wouldn't miss it."

"Could you watch Diesel instead?" I ask. "He's supposed to stay quiet, so I don't want to bring him."

No! Diesel whimpers. *I must come!* He stands up and licks at my face.

"Wow, he's pretty active for a wounded dog. That'll be some job," Morgan answers. "But sure, I can stay with Diesel."

No, no, no! Diesel barks. *All of the pack must come!* "Rouff!"

"I've never seen him so worked up," Morgan says. "You would think he knows what we're talking about."

"You'd be surprised." I frown and try to clear my head of Diesel's voice so I can think.

I will save you. Diesel shuffles, then barks again.

"You need to be quiet!" I tell him.

He pants heavily now. His eyes glint. *We need the whole pack.*

I sigh. Trouble is, I don't entirely understand what Diesel knows. "Oh, what the heck. We have to bring Baby Luanne anyway. Might as well bring Diesel. We'll just take it way easy."

"Tom and Simon and the others might be hanging out at the dock in front of Zorba's. I heard there's even free ice cream tomorrow. We can give your folks alone time. No Frisbee chasing, don't worry."

At the dock in front of Zorba's. Free ice cream. An icicle of fear shoots down my spine, and I feel hot and cold at the same time. I won't go there. No way. Maybe the drowning was only a dream, but I'm not going to tempt fate. My vision can't come true, not without my co-operation. And I will *not* co-operate.

That night poor Diesel can't get under the bed with his cone on. *My head won't fit.*

I fold up my top blanket and place it on the floor for him and he circles it a few times. Finally he lies down but can't find a comfy way to put his head down. Instead, he sits. In the dim light, I watch as his eyes close.

Cone thing in the way. He still won't lay his head on the blanket.

I get up and help him, tugging his collar gently. His eyes flick open, a sleepy toffee gaze. "You can do it. I know it's not comfy but … Here, I'll come sleep down there with you." I place my pillow on the floor beside him and pull a blanket over us.

Better! His chest heaves with a big sigh.

When I drape my hand across his back, I can feel Dad's faulty gift watch between us. I reach to unbuckle it.

Don't take off the time counter! Diesel lifts his head and looks straight into my eyes. *It is our life counter.* Diesel licks his lips like he's trying to sound the words out loud.

I show the watch face to him as though he can tell time. Maybe he can. *But it's not counting anything.*

I have told you: when you are safe, it will start again. He looks away and gives a one-note whine.

"But what does that really mean?" I gently turn his head to make him look my way again. "What do you know?"

I cannot tell until after. I made a promise.

"Till after what?" I ask him. This is all so crazy. What does Diesel know?

He whines another note. *Till after you are safe.*

25

Thursday, July 1:

Disaster Picnic

Next morning, I awake on the floor, my arm across Diesel, and remember his thoughts from last night. An idea I was mulling over suddenly becomes sharp as a photograph. *Do you really mean if we make it past four thirty today, time will start again and we'll be safe?*

Yes.

But why?

He only gazes back at me with his melty brown eyes and whines once.

A knock at the door interrupts us, making me sit up. Mom peeks in without waiting.

"Time to get up, Naomi. Get some breakfast and then pack up the bathroom medicine cabinet."

I wipe at the sleep in my eyes. "What about the picnic?" I'm hoping we don't go anywhere near Hamilton Beach. Better chance of us staying safe that way.

"That reminds me. Check the dishes box your father packed. I think he stuffed the red tablecloth in there," Mom answers. "We'll take that."

Her head disappears.

Toast! Toast! Diesel barks.

I blink at him.

He barks some more. *Hurry!*

But why? We could stay home. I wouldn't drown. No car could come near you.

We can't do that. Don't worry. I will save you. I will save the pack! He begins barking again. *Hurry, hurry.*

"Okay, okay!" I dress quickly and we head to the kitchen together.

When we pass them, Mom and Dad are taking down pictures from the wall. "I'm going to chuck this ballerina print," Dad says. "There's a crack in the glass."

"But my mother gave us that one."

"Exactly," he answers. "And nobody in this house does ballet. Do you like it, Adele?"

"I don't hate it. I definitely want to get rid of this fish, though." Mom has always found the stuffed bass hanging in the hallway gruesome. Dad caught it on one of his trips up north with the gang from United Steelworks.

"Stuffed fish and cracked ballet print, good riddance." Dad dusts his fingertips against each other. Compromising over bad art seems like a good sign. But after we're finished our breakfast, toast and kibble, I notice both wall hangings sitting in the keeper box.

As I empty the medicine cabinet, I hear Dad blathering about how good this move is for everyone, family working together, helping each other.

Mom answers in short clips. "As you say." "Whatever you want." "Your idea." For her it's a funeral; for him it's a party.

By the time Aunt Cathie comes with Baby Luanne, I've packed my share and Mom's shoulders are hunched and her arms are folded across her chest. Not a good sign.

Dad whistles as he hitches Luanne's car seat into the Neon, but Mom stays quiet except to say goodbye to Aunt Cathie.

Then Dad baby-talks with Luanne as he carries her to the car. I walk more slowly behind him with Diesel, still in his space collar. Mom carries the red tablecloth. We drive to Morgan's to pick her up, and she squeezes me into the middle of the backseat. Diesel stretches across both of us, panting so that his drool rolls along the white plastic funnel to my bare legs. I don't even mind anymore. Not much anyway.

I want to stick my head out the window. To catch the wind with my mouth, Diesel tells me.

Sorry, Diesel. No telling what the wind will do with that cone around your neck. I scrub around his ears.

As we drive the scenic route along the lake, Canadian flags wave at us from every house, bright red signs of the holiday. Dad chats about how pretty the homes are. "Maybe we can rent one here next year. Or even buy one. Look at that house that looks like a castle. That could be ours."

"Dreamer," my mother mutters.

Morgan raises her eyebrows in alarm at me.

The more nervous Dad gets, the more his mouth motors, and that engine works about as well as the Neon's, which stalls twice. "Slated for a tune-up Tuesday," Dad tells us cheerily.

We pull into a space right near a gap in the trees. Perfect. A picnic table sits underneath the shade of a mulberry. Just beyond it the blue of the lake stretches out for an eternity.

I can believe anything, looking at that blue. Can Mom?

Getting Diesel out of the car takes a bit of wrangling and lots of scratches on our bare legs from his nails and collar. I unbuckle Luanne but slide out on Morgan's side as Mom lifts Luanne out. Dad pops the trunk and hauls out a beat-up old cooler.

Diesel scrambles over, ears perked. *Alpha Male brought the food box?*

"You actually brought a picnic?" Mom seems just as surprised.

"Well, yes. Much as I enjoy the fish and chips here, I know how you like my egg salad."

"You made us sandwiches?" Mom's eyes pop wide as Dad carries the cooler to the table.

Cold bread with meat stuffing? Diesel barks.

"Egg salad," I correct Diesel out loud.

"Yes, I didn't know if Luanne could eat eggs yet, so I brought her a banana and some yogurt." He plunks the cooler on the picnic bench.

On the blue expanse of water, I spot sailboats, four of them, white-winged dancers skimming the lake. All different than the way it happened last time. I breathe a little easier.

"Did you bake something for dessert?" Morgan asks.

I elbow her.

Mom spreads the red tablecloth over the grey wood.

"No," Dad says. "For dessert I thought I would treat everyone to an ice cream cone. Nothing quite as delicious on a hot day."

Icy, creamy, tasty stuff! Diesel pants happily. *The pack celebrates.*

Dad reaches inside the cooler and pulls out a bunch of daisies in a plastic pop bottle. They look a bit wilted, half sad, half cheery, like Dad's attempt at being romantic. She loves you, she loves you not. "These are for you," he tells Mom.

Diesel's head tilts. *Do these blossoms taste good?*

"Just pretty," I answer out loud.

"Like your mom," Dad answers, as if I were talking to him.

Mom smiles as she sets the bottle of daisies on the table.

Dad pulls out more of those cheap paper plates he used at Uncle Leo's cookout and piles the sandwiches on top. The sandwiches looked slightly squished in the middle. He takes out Luanne's banana and yogurt and a roll of paper towel. From the bottom of the cooler he lifts out a bag of baby carrots and a plastic container of grape tomatoes. Vegetables? Opens them up and dumps them on one of his paper plates. Then he pours white sparkling grape juice into plastic glasses for all of us.

"Ladies, and dog, I have an announcement to make. Just recently I completed bus driver training and the required Saint John's Ambulance course —"

"Does that mean you can perform artificial resuscitation on a dead person?" Morgan asks.

I elbow her a second time, harder. She is interrupting his big speech.

"Yes, it does, Morgan, among many other things, like the upper thrust, wound management, and general first aid, all usually performed on live people." He looks around at us and raises his glass to start again: "Wednesday, I passed my B-class driver's licence. Starting September I will be driving a school bus for the morning and afternoon run."

"Yay!" I pump a fist into the air.

"Hurray!" Morgan cheers, too.

"Rouff!" Diesel joins in.

But Mom doesn't seem excited at all. "A couple bus routes a day? That won't provide a living wage."

"No. But there's a nice signing bonus. And there will be charters. I'll continue to work shifts in between at Western

Tire. I can bring Luanne on my bus rides as long as I supply the car seat. Your sister will save on daycare."

"That will be nice for Cathie." Mom's smile straightens.

"Oh, and I have plans. Once I have experience, I can apply for a full-time position driving a city bus. Or I can go for my airbrakes licence so I can drive a truck."

"You *are* a good driver," Mom admits.

"Yes, I am. Let's raise our grape juice to a new chapter in our lives."

"Our lives?" Mom's eyebrows do a jumping jack.

Morgan and I quickly raise our glasses. "Cheers!" Morgan says.

"To a new life!" I yell. Or my old life back, complete with a dad and a dog.

The whole pack! "Rawf!"

Even Luanne wants to clink plastic. Or maybe the sound is more of a click. Her baby fingers clutch around her sippy cup and she reaches out her dimpled arm as far as she can.

We all meet it with our glasses and she giggles.

Only Mom hesitates. "I'm not sure how you think this will change things for us."

"To start, I'll be able to make support payments in full and on time," Dad says. He clicks his glass with hers before she even raises it. Then he chugs his bubbly grape quickly and gives a long "Ahhh!"

She just looks at him, not drinking any.

"But I'd also like to put my family back together again," Dad says.

That nursery rhyme suddenly comes to me: *All the king's horses and all the king's men couldn't put Humpty together again.* Not even Dad's egg salad.

"Just think. If we all live together with Cathie, we'll be saving money on rent. You could start taking college courses like you wanted."

Mom shakes her head. I'm not sure if she's in shock or it's a flat-out no. She stares at her glass for a while and then, finally, drinks.

Morgan wolfs down her sandwich. "This is great egg salad. What's your secret, James?"

I wince when she calls Dad by his first name, even if she is trying to be nice.

"I finely chop the eggs and celery. Add a good squeeze of real lemon juice. And then I use the best mayonnaise possible. None of this low-fat stuff. Better to have quality than quantity." Dad's mouth is still motoring. Sputtering, stalling, like his Neon.

I finish eating my sandwich and lick my fingers. "The world could use more fat." I smile at my mother.

She stares at me, blankly.

I take a carrot from the plate. Morgan pops a grape tomato into her mouth.

"This isn't just about having money," Mom finally tells my father.

"Hey, Dad, do you want us to go get ice cream now?" I don't want to hear this. It sounds like my advice to him was wrong and Dad's efforts will all be for nothing.

Diesel whines his sad one-note. Even he agrees.

"Yes, the girls should go. We need to talk about this alone," Mom says.

"Sure, go and get your ice cream now." Dad pulls out his wallet and hands me three twenties. "That's for the gas the other day. You don't have to bring me any change. Just buy Morgan and Baby Luanne whatever they want, too."

"Okay, Dad." I pick up Diesel's leash, and Morgan pushes the stroller. We walk slowly away, the sand clogging up the stroller wheels.

"You could take Diesel off his leash," Morgan suggests. "There aren't any cars on the beach."

She's right and Diesel is miserable enough with that stupid white satellite around his head. I reach under the plastic to unsnap the leash.

"He's walking pretty good for a dog who got hit by a car last night," Morgan says cheerily.

At least I still have my dog. I smile. "Yeah, he's limber all right."

Dog yoga, remember? Diesel bends down onto his front paws.

"No. Stop that, Diesel!" Morgan holds up a finger for him to pay attention. "No playing — you're supposed to be resting!" She shakes that finger at him. Then we continue on.

Despite the bumpy ride, or maybe because of it, Luanne's head bobs down and she falls asleep. Another thing I should be happy about.

For a few minutes the slap of our flip-flops against the soles of our feet is the only sound we make — till we're far enough away from the picnic table.

Then Morgan starts.

"You don't think we should have stayed to help your dad's case? It didn't look like he was winning your mom over."

"What do you know? Egg salad is her favourite." I feel like kicking Morgan because she's right. Dad's losing.

"That was a great sandwich. Ya gotta give him that." *Slap, slap!*

"He's going to babysit Luanne while driving a bus. What more does Mom want?" *Slap, slap!*

"She's a demanding woman with no sense of humour." *Slap, slap!*

"What did you say?" My feet stop moving.

"I just meant that what he was doing should have worked." She stops beside me.

"What do you know? My dad is unreliable. He said he'd teach me to swim this summer but he never did. He was short on his support money, so we have to move. His car stalls at every corner even though he works part-time at a garage."

"You really can't count on him."

"I can't count on anyone!" I realize then that I really don't want Morgan to agree with anything I'm saying. "Just shut up!" I run ahead.

Pack fight! Diesel barks.

"She's not part of the pack!" I yell.

"What are you talking about?" Morgan ploughs the stroller through the sand to catch up. Luanne's head bobs up.

"Nothing, nothing. I'm not talking to you. I'm talking to the dog!"

26

Thursday, July 1:

Losing Diesel

Our flip-flops keep slapping, but I can't talk to Morgan anymore. I've got nothing left to say. Luanne settles back into a deeper sleep.

Diesel stops and whines suddenly. I look in the direction he's looking. Ahead of us the dock stretches into the lake. Approaching it is broad-shouldered, good-looking Simon. He's holding Su-Ling's hand.

I groan and put my head in my hand.

"He'll drop her by September, don't worry. You'll get another chance."

"Did you not hear me? *Shut up!*"

Diesel barks. *Wiener Girl should be part of the pack.*

"I don't care! She's not!" Again, I say that out loud.

Morgan stops walking, tilts her head, and squints at me. "Are you all right?"

"No!" I start running and then stumble to my knees.

Diesel barks a few times. *Come swim!*

I feel too miserable to look up. Everything is going wrong. I'm never going to grow tall enough to be anything but a peanut to the kids at school. But worse than that, Dad and Mom are never getting back together. Morgan was right.

Diesel keeps barking. *Swimming birds. I will catch one for us.* Then I hear a splash and another and another.

"Diesel, no!" Morgan calls, and finally I get up.

"Come back, Diesel!" I yell after him.

A couple of fat green mallards bob along the waves. Diesel gallops through the water toward them. But his funnel collar fills up with water. He doesn't seem to realize it right away. He paddles a few metres from shore and then a wave tosses him over.

He yelps. *Neck thing hurts!*

"Diesel, get out of there!"

He rights himself. His legs churn and he continues following the ducks. Farther and farther out. But the collar pulls his head down.

I can't stay up.

"Diesel!" I scream.

"Naomi, we have to help him." Morgan parks the stroller at the water's edge, then tears off her shirt and shorts.

I stand frozen. She doesn't understand. I can't go out there. I will be acting out my death scene a second time. Only this time, Diesel and I will both drown.

"Let's jump off the dock. We'll reach him faster." Morgan doesn't even wait. She starts running.

I look at the waves. If anything they are higher than the first time. The sailboats are white specks in the distance. Nobody else stands on the dock. I look to the shore for help. Simon and Su-Ling sit on the patio of Zorba's sipping umbrella drinks, not looking our way. I check on Luanne. Still deep asleep.

My watch flashes *4:30* as always. No time left if I want to save Diesel. I pull off my shorts and top and chase after Morgan.

Diesel flounders in the waves. He doesn't bark or yelp, but I hear his thoughts. *So tired. Can't stay up anymore. Must catch swimming bird.*

Morgan's feet pound on the dock. "Hurry, Naomi!"

My feet hit the wood and I follow Morgan to the end.

She turns to me, holding out her hand.

I feel that icicle along my spine again. I look at my watch. "I can't do it. I can't swim."

"You can too! We have to save Diesel."

I shake my head. Lift it to see a wave sweeping over him.

"Take my hand. Trust me!" Morgan's grey eyes lock on to mine.

Trust, trust. Am I just imagining Diesel's thoughts inside my head?

I blink and look down at her fingers, which are waving impatiently.

We can save our whole pack together.

I sigh and grab at them. We both jump in.

The water smacks me like a wet hand, burning into my nose and making me cough.

"Swim underwater but stay with me," Morgan says.

The water looks green, much darker than the pool, but I allow myself to sink, then follow Morgan's glowing white legs. We swim and swim till I need to come up for air. Diesel flounders just a metre away.

"Make sure to lift his head up. I'll get his back."

I've got your back — her famous saying. Now she will have my dog's. I move slower on top of the water. I catch a mouthful of water and cough again.

"Don't panic. We only have to swim a little more and then we can walk him in."

I push myself forward. Still able to breathe, still in control. But Diesel looks limp, like roadkill in the water. I gulp and push harder.

"We're almost there. I've got his hips."

I wrap my arm around his shoulders. His head feels too heavy. My other arm stretches ahead; my knees fold and then straighten behind me. Once, twice …

"Oh my god. Luanne, stay in the stroller!" Morgan suddenly calls.

I look up in time to see her tumble out and scramble to her feet. "No, baby. Don't come in the water!"

She giggles and toddles forward.

"You don't have your water wings on. Go back!" I yell.

She keeps coming. She's up to her knees now. A wave hits her and she stops for a moment, looking startled. When the second one hits, she falls backward.

She isn't laughing now. She isn't making a sound. She's not even trying to get up.

"Dad!" I scream. "Mom!" I wave. They are so far away.

Dad suddenly turns and looks. He jumps to his feet, points, and yells to Mom. They break into a run. Dad's a former track star, and his legs stretch long like a giraffe's. Can he make it in time?

I can't chance it. Heart in my mouth, I let go of Diesel and rush to Luanne. In five strides, I duck down and scoop her out of the water. She sputters and then wails.

Turning back, I see Morgan dragging Diesel, but his head hangs limp in that water-filled cone. Morgan sobs.

Can I leave Baby Luanne on the shore and rush back to help? Or is it too big a risk?

I shuffle Luanne to my hip and run till the water chokes my legs. Then I sink down with Luanne, and as Morgan comes closer with Diesel I reach under the stupid plastic cone with my free hand and prop up his head.

I've got you, Diesel. You're okay. Hang in there, boy.

"Your father's coming to help!" Morgan says.

I have to leave you now, Diesel says.

No, Diesel. Stay with me. We crab-crawl forward as fast as we can.

Dad runs in and takes Luanne from my arm. "There, there, baby. Don't cry!"

He turns and gives Luanne to Mom.

"Diesel, wake up!" I beg as we fall down exhausted on the wet sand.

Why did you chase those stupid ducks? You should know better! You'll see.

Dad kneels down beside us. He unbuckles Diesel's collar, removing the white satellite with it.

I got you another chance. I made you listen. You have your pack.

Diesel looks dead.

Dad takes Diesel's front paw and hold his thumb against the underside. "I'm getting something. Not sure how strong a dog's pulse should be."

You got me another chance? I ask Diesel inside my head.

I should have been there to save you the first time.

But how did you get the chance?

I asked the all-knowing one. On the other side.

Dad rolls Diesel to his right side.

The all-knowing one? You were dead!

But I begged to have enough life back so I could save you.

I feel a weight sink inside me. *So the bargain is up because I'm saved? No!* "Diesel, stay with me. Please!" I beg out loud.

It's over. I've saved you and the pack.

"Please!"

"I'm trying my best." Dad forces Diesel's mouth open, moving his tongue out of the way. Then he straightens

Diesel's head and holds his fingers around his snout to close his mouth.

I glance down at my wrist. The numbers haven't budged. Maybe I can't change a thing after all.

"Wow," Morgan gasps. "Your dad sure knows what he's doing. Mouth-to-mouth on a dog!"

Mouth-to-nose actually. *Diesel, come back! Tell me what it's like.*

I ca-an't!

Dad leans over and blows into Diesel's nostrils. I see Diesel's chest rise and fall. Two, three, and four more breaths.

And again. Once, twice. Each time Diesel's chest rises and falls, but his eyes stayed closed. Three times, four. Once, twice …

"Ack, ack, ack!" Diesel's eyes pop open as he coughs and throws up a puddle of water.

"He's breathing!" Dad leans back.

Diesel's front paws wave a bit. Unbelievably, his tail flaps. He struggles to his feet.

"Easy, boy. Take it easy." Dad rubs his fur gently.

I reach to pat him, too. "Down, Diesel. Stay."

He doesn't move. He fixes his toffee eyes on me. It's such a knowing, soulful look. But he doesn't think anything inside my head.

"You're safe!" I pat him. "We're all safe."

Dad stands up, and Mom falls into his arms, Luanne squeezed between them. He strokes Mom's hair.

Diesel's mouth drops open. Looks almost like a grin. I lean in close to him.

C'mon, Diesel. Tell me what it's like on the other side. What is the all-knowing one like? A man, a woman? A dog?

He wags his tail and licks my face.

You're never going to talk to me again, are you?

More licks. No thoughts.

"He sure looks happy for someone who nearly drowned." Crouching down beside me, Morgan scratches at his ears.

Mom is kissing Dad now.

"Rawf!" Diesel's not saying anything inside my head, but his dimples show.

Morgan watches my parents. "Saving the dog worked way better than making egg-salad sandwiches."

"Sandwiches had nothing to do with it — it's all about the eggs," I say.

Morgan looks at me strangely, but I just wink at her. Maybe Diesel has put my parents back together again.

A long shadow falls over us and I look up. Simon. "That was some pretty amazing life saving. Your father, Morgan, and you," — Simon hesitates for a moment, looks directly into my eyes, and says my name as though tasting it — "Naomi."

"And she just learned how to swim, too," Morgan adds, and I want to slug her.

Simon kneels down beside us and I feel the flop, flop of Diesel's tail against my leg, dog applause. "You," he says, patting Diesel's head, "sure get into a lot of trouble."

Diesel keeps panting, that big dog grin across his snout.

Simon stands up again. "We're lining up on the other side of the restaurant. They're giving away free ice cream if you want to join us."

"I think we're good. We had a big lunch."

Diesel barks a one-note goodbye. At least that's what I think it is. Simon heads back toward Su-Ling.

"Just wait till September," Morgan says.

Diesel looks pretty satisfied with himself. As though he nearly drowned on purpose to bring the pack together. As though he knew all along he would lose the ability to talk to me inside my head.

That's all right. He doesn't have to lay it all out for me. I understand. He talked me into adding Morgan to the pack. He showed Mom just how terrific Dad can be.

As long as you don't run in front of a car, I'm okay with you not talking.

"You're a smart dog," I tell him, and his tail flings up sand.

"I wish dogs could talk," Morgan tells me. "I wonder what he would say."

"Rawf!"

"You can't hear what he's saying?" I smile at Diesel.

"I don't speak bark."

I look at my watch. "It's four forty! Do you see this? My watch is running!"

"Yippee. Time to get a cellphone like the rest of the world."

"It's four forty," I tell Diesel. I lift his ear. "We're safe," I say softly. "But you knew that."

No words from him, inside or outside my head. "We've survived." I stare into his eyes. Still no thoughts.

We're back to being an ordinary dog and owner. Watching Diesel's body wag, I try to imagine what he could be thinking. *Hurray, we will enjoy more toast together! And walkies! We can play with the flat disc. We can swim. I love my pack!*

I don't need words. Diesel is all about life's simple pleasures. I glance down at my watch again. It's four forty-one now, and we are both safe, the most important thing.

"Rawf!" He sure seems to agree.

"That makes twice we saved his life … together," Morgan says.

"Rawf!"

"Thanks, Morgan!" *Trust, trust.* Not his thoughts, just some memory of what Diesel once told me.

Diesel licks Morgan's face and then turns toward me.

Come on, Diesel. Tell me just one more thing. Did you plan it like this? Almost drown yourself to make Dad look like a hero?

He doesn't think anything loud enough for me to hear, but I have a feeling about all that's happened, and I trust that feeling.

Acknowledgements

Starting with David Bennett, who always loved this story, through to my current, wonderful agent Amy Thompson, I'm grateful for all the attention and support along the way.

To Scott Fraser, Kathryn Lane, and Jenny McWha, thank you for choosing to accompany me on the publishing journey again; to Laura Boyle, for another beautiful cover; and to Susan Fitzgerald, for working to fix the little nits with me.

To the larger creative community of CANSCAIP (Canadian Society of Children's Authors and Performers) thank you for giving me such a feeling of connection and belonging. Finally, thank you to my many writing friends who critique and applaud all my work: Lynda Simmons, Rachael Preston, Jennifer Mook-Sang, Jennifer Maruno, Claudia White, Anitha Rao-Robinson, Lyn Leitch, Natalie Hyde, Deborah Serravalle, Gillian Chan, Sharon E. McKay, Lana Button, Lucy Falcone, and Karen Bass. I'm so happy to know you "have my back."

About the Author

Sylvia McNicoll is an acclaimed arts educator and author of over thirty-five novels, many published internationally. She won the Ontario Library Association Silver Birch and the Manitoba Young Readers' Choice Award in 1996 for *Bringing Up Beauty*, her dog guide–raising story. In 2013, her young adult novel *Crush.Candy.Corpse.* was shortlisted for the Crime Writers of Canada Best Crime Juvenile/YA Book, the OLA Red Maple, the Manitoba Young Readers' Choice, and the Saskatchewan Snow Willow, and it continues to be considered the definitive book on Alzheimer's for teens. She is also the author of *Last Chance for Paris*, *Best Friends Through Eternity*, *Revenge on the Fly*, *Body Swap*, and the Great Mistake Mystery series. Sylvia currently lives with her husband and Jackapoo, Mortie, in Burlington, Ontario.